HYPOCRITES

The sculpture reproduced on the endpaper depicts a scene where three soothsayers are interpreting to King Suddhodana the dream of Queen Maya, mother of Lord Buddha. Below them is seated a scribe recording the interpretation. This is perhaps the earliest available pictorial record of the art of writing in India.

From Nagarjunakonda, 2nd century A.D.

Courtesy: National Museum, New Delhi

SAHITYA AKADEMI AWARD-WINNING
RAJASTHANI NOVEL

HYPOCRITES

Meva ra Roonkh

ANNA RAM 'SUDAMA'

Translated from the original Rajasthani
by
Nagarmal Sahal

Sahitya Akademi

Hypocrites: English translation by Nagarmal Sahal of Anna Ram 'Sudama's' Akademi Award-winning Rajasthani novel *Meva ra Roonkh.* Sahitya Akademi, New Delhi, 1997

Sahitya Akademi

Head Office

Rabindra Bhavan, 35 Ferozeshah Road, New Delhi 110 001

Sales Section, 'Swati', Mandir Marg, New Delhi 110 001

Regional Offices

Jeevan Tara Building, 23A/44X, Diamond Harbour Road, Taratala, Calcutta 700 053

ADA Rangamandira, 109, J.C. Road, Bangalore 560 002

172, Mumbai Marathi Grantha Sangrahalaya Marg, Dadar, Mumbai 400 014

Chennai Office

Guna Building, II Floor, 304-305 Anna Salai, Teynampet, Chennai 600 018

First published, 1997

ISBN 81-260-0234-4

Rs.

Typeset by S.J.I. Services, New Delhi 110024 and printed at Tara Art Printers, Noida.

1

Sinath said to his cousin, Sugana, "Come on, get up now. Don't you see the sun has risen? Tear yourself away from your *chilam** and come out. We must complete one of the earmarked rows before the first meal comes out to us at the field." Sugana put down his *chilam* and came out.

"Cover it with sand, lest a spark sets off a fire..."

"Relax, brother, that won't happen."

"Don't be so smug," said Sinath. "It's good that no such mishap has occurred so far but who knows when it may, and catch us unaware? Anyway get the pickaxes from the hut." Sugana simply nodded.

With pickaxes on their shoulders, sandy towels around their barebodies and with their *dhotis* raised above their knees, the cousins trotted off to weed the field, like soldiers marching off to a battle-front.

"Sugana, why don't you give up smoking? Can smoke fill an empty stomach?"

"I know the saying that both back-biting and smoking are pernicious habits. But you know," Sugana said after a while, "on his death-bed my grandfather gave me his *hookah*. He used to love me a lot. I used to prepare his *hookah* and now, I have become a victim of this habit. However, since you disapprove of it so strongly, I give it up here and now. Such a nasty thing can do no good. And it can't cleanse the body either."

---

* An earthen or metallic vessel on the top of a hubble-bubble containing the fire and tobacco.

"It really does not matter much. But what if a spark from it sets afire our hut while we are away. This is, after all, our precious little storehouse."

"No hut or cottage can be more valuable than our lives," said Sugana. "What is bad can never become good."

Talking to each other, they reached the field and began work in right earnest. Sinath was about thirty-five years old and Sugana was five years younger to him. Even though they did not live in a joint family, their land was cultivated jointly. Sinath was a matriculate and was quite rich in mother-wit.

The field was rich with grain and needed a good rain to save the plants from wilting. Some imbecile plants had already given up and died. The sorry state of the crop saddened Sinath. If it didn't rain within a week, all their plants would die, flattened against the soil. They would be left with nothing. The sheer thought of it made Sinath shiver with apprehension. No less than five maunds of seed had been sown but who could have foreseen such a drought? He looked at the sun. It was scorching, though it was yet so early. There was no wind and it was excruciatingly hot. The earth was parched. In ten minutes or so he was wet with sweat. The weather would take the very life out of him. Just then, he luckily observed a happy indication of forthcoming rain. To his left, in the shade of a tree, a few birds were frisking and bathing in the sand. Though he really did not have much faith in this sign, the twitter of the birds steadied him a little and his pain and sadness receded.

He looked at the boundary of his field, about fifty feet away, and noticed some stray animals inside it. He shouted, "Sugana, just run and turn those animals out. Their owners don't look after them and do not even bother about their whereabouts."

Sugana ran towards them, his axe in hand. Sinath shouted behind him, warning him not to use his axe against the cows. Going back to weeding with his pick-axe, Sinath muttered to himself, "These stray animals will not let us live in peace. We must have a thorny hedge to cover all the openings." He had such a practised pair of hands that he could weed the field without even looking at them and harming the plants growing right next to them. There was little chance of his going amiss. He had weeded for less than an hour when he saw his mother and children coming with the food. He went on working for another ten minutes. Both the cousins then went to the little shack and settled down to their morning meal. There were *rotis*, some buttermilk, a few onions and salt and chillies knotted in a rag. His mother said, "You have to make do with this poor stuff, but in a month or so, when our buffalo gives birth to a calf, you will have plenty of buttermilk to your heart's content. Till then we have no other go. Even onions are being sold by the grocer Dhanna at the rate of two-and-a-half rupees a kilo."

"What? Two-and-a-half rupees!"

"Yes, and even then he cheats on the weight."

"But since when have onions become so indispensable? We are Jats and cannot afford to be fastidious in our eating habits. For now we can surely manage with just chillies in salt and water to serve as our vegetable."

"My son, chillies are equally dear. They cost between ten and twelve rupees a kilo. And the quality is miserable. They are all mixed with rubbish, and the weight is invariably short. We can relish our *rotis* more with just four peels of onions."

Sinath's father arrived at the field, his axe on his shoulder; bare-bodied with a dusty towel tightly wound round his head. He was a short man, in his sixties and had a small beard. The furrows on his forehead told of a long and painful life.

He sensed the nature of their conversation and said, "In the city onions are being sold for two rupees a kilo, whereas in the month of *Jeth* one could have two-and-a-half kilos for just a rupee. Dhania, that clever businessman, purchased a load which he stored in an inner room of his house. He must not have paid more than a rupee for three kilos. He sold them at the rate of two or two-and-a-half rupees a kilo. What shall a poor man eat and wear? It is easier to simply breathe one's last, rather than to spend more than one's means and to pass through a crisis of this magnitude."

"Dhania will not be content even if he earns seven times his expenses," Sinath mumbled, his mouth full of food. "Even then he is prone to give short weight. The inefficient administration dare not take any action against these errant shopkeepers."

"My dear son, don't you know that birds of the same feather flock together? The administration is simply non-existent. Their one and only concern is money. They beg for our votes assuring us of their unstinted support and help. But blood is thicker than water. Instead of serving us, they rather end up serving their own kith and kin. Had their mothers given birth to them with a spirit of service, they would have raised stairs to the sky. This earth will be fortunate indeed if altruistic persons were ever to be born. Forget about service and help, we will thank our stars if they let us live as we are and not strangle us to death."

The old man went to the metal vessel which was kept out of the sun, and drank water from the cup formed by joining his palms together. After taking two gulps of water he said, "The water today is not as cold as before. So the rain must be approaching fast. The saying goes:

'If the water is warm in a pitcher,
And birds bathe in sand,
If ants with their eggs ascend,
There should be ample rains.'"

This appealed so much to Sinath that his heart became lighter. His father, axe in hand, went off to weed the field. Sinath wanted to tell his father about Sugana's resolve to give up smoking, but his father was already some distance away, and this news could very well wait. The two brothers had not yet finished their meal. They were dipping their *rotis* in buttermilk when they heard the loud engine sound of a jeep. Leaving their *thalis* behind and their fingers unlicked they ran off, the food still clinging to their lips. They threw themselves down in a trench at the western boundary. The women hid themselves in the hut and the old man crouched where he was. Only when the sound had died down did they come out of hiding. They saw the jeep in the distance, speeding towards the village. The danger was past and the cousins resumed their unfinished meal.

The old man said, "What a time this is and what strange things are happening before our very eyes. Will they let us live? They just grab anyone they come across irrespective of age, whether sixteen or sixty. They sterilized poor Rawatia Meghwal. Prabhu's grandson was going to the city with a load of chopped grass and cattle-fodder. A policeman grabbed him and got him vasectomized."

Sugana said that he had been betrothed only the other day. The old man interjected, "This dishonest lot, with their madness to sterilize us men, have made the very institution of marriage unnecessary. The poor people protest but to no avail. Tell me who can tell the elephant that he has turned rogue?"

"Grandpa, we have heard that the villagers, even the old men and women, armed with axes, lathis and even kitchen knives, stood before the government jeep saying that they would kill and be killed if need be, but they would not allow anybody to touch them. We heard that the government staff had to turn back never to return again."

"Not many people are bold enough to face death. It's never easy to oppose the government, but if we all resist unitedly, it would certainly be a serious crisis for the government. But there is no such possibility in the near future. If they sow wind today, they are bound to reap the whirlwind tomorrow. It is obvious that their sins have reached their height. Injustice can never prevail for long."

The old man returned to his weeding and the two cousins enjoyed their siesta in the shade of a Khejari tree.

They had just lain down and had hardly changed their sides when they saw Kanha, the officer-in-charge of the police station, approach. Sinath sat up and said, "Welcome, Kotwal. So, tell us some of the village gossip."

Taking a deep breath he sat down and said, "You know all that's going on in the village."

"I have not been there for the last ten days. This land is good enough for us," said Sinath.

"That is how you have weeded about thirty ploughs without spending a single pie. You two brothers work like machines. My four-plough piece is lying unweeded and uncared for."

"How can you manage? You are on the wrong side of fifty-five years. Moreover, you have grown weak. But you have your son and his hefty wife to help you."

This saddened the Kotwal. Tears trickled down his cheeks and disappeared in his beard. He did not speak a word.

"Kanha, Why do you hesitate to open your heart to us? Tell us frankly how we can help you."

"You have always been my benefactor," Kanha said. "Haven't I always in the past told you of my joys and sorrows? When our police station was disbanded, it was you who saw me through. The good done even once is not to be slighted or forgotten."

"Then why not come out with your tale of woe?"

"My son's wife is no good. His second marriage has proved ruinous to us. They wasted all the money and have ruined me. This alone is my sore point which worries me greatly."

"If you find it difficult to make both ends meet then we could lend you some grain. Why do you worry?"

"Food is no problem. The problem is my daughter-in-law who has crossed all limits. She needs soaps, perfumes, scents and essences in such abundance as though she were some rich man's wife."

"But she must be doing something."

"She pats cow-dung into cakes at the Seth's residence, cleans the portico and thus earns a living. She returns home whenever she pleases. All the young louts and other vagabonds of the village keep on hanging around the house, leering at her. How can I drive them out when she herself indulges them?"

"Shall I try to bring your son round?"

"No, no. We would be happy indeed if he were good. To add to my misery, he drinks and keeps the company of rogues and ruffians."

"The world is a school for scandal. They take malicious pleasure in slandering others," said Sinath.

"No, your grace, one may make a mountain of a molehill, but when there is no molehill it is not..."

"Yes, true it is, these days."

"Anyway, enough said. Let me go to my field. Who knows, it may yet yield two maunds of grain. Sharing my grief with you has lightened my heart."

Sinath watched Kanha's face intently and could read his growing anxiety. His wrinkled face betrayed restlessness. Changing the topic he said, "It seems that a jeep has gone towards the village."

"Yes, I forgot to tell you. Some policemen have come to the village today."

"What for?"

"Day before yesterday, Gango, the potter, was returning from the field with a load of dung-cakes on his ass. Near the boundary, Shaitan Singh accosted him with a stick. He abused the potter saying, 'You bring dung-cakes from our field but when we ask you for a pitcher, you don't pay any heed. Does the farm belong to your father? We pay tax, and you want to grab the profit!' Shaitan hit Gango twice in the face. The poor potter went home sobbing. Many people gathered at his house.

"What happened then?"

"Some of them took him to the police-station. Since they reported the case, the police were bound to make an appearance. In the village there are many agents of the police Sub-Inspector. They feed him well to better their interest."

"Yes, and then?"

"Something very interesting happened. Many sturdy people were standing around. When they heard the sound of the jeep, somebody said that the vasectomy staff were coming. Everyone ran helter-skelter and none was left behind.

Sinath was about to say that he too would have done the same but desisted. The Kotwal drank some water and left.

The two brothers resumed work. In the distance some women were digging out thorny grass. It was then that Sinath's mother came up to them. "I would like to go to the village," she said. "The girls should not be left alone."

Sinath said, "Ma, so early? How is Moolki?"

"Who knows if she will live or die. Her eyes are dull and her face is bloodless and pale. She is but twelve years old, and even then she seems to have been sucked dry. Meghli is running a temperature today. What about you?"

"I shall come tomorrow after the weeding is done."

"The head priest of Ramdwara is ill and many people were around to have his *darshana*."

"Is he seriously ill?"

"This is what we have heard but I cannot say for sure."

"Then I must not put off my visit till tomorrow. I must see him at the earliest," said Sinath.

Sinath seemed a little worried for a while. He mused, "I need not think of the future. I must concentrate on the present." He then resumed his work.

Enraged with the activities of the ignorant world and tired with the whole day's exertion, the sun took shelter in a bed of clouds and was no more visible. The western sky seemed immersed in a red lake which indicated the setting sun's ire. There was no wind and it was much too sultry. The fields seemed silent and melancholy, waiting as they were for the rains. Farms were enveloped in darkness. The air was filled with the twitter of birds, flying back to their nests and the cawing of crows. The sound of flocks of sheep returning to their steads and the ringing melody of the moving bullock-carts created new *Ragas*. But Sinath and Sugana did not hear them—they were busy mending the wicket- gates. Breaking the silence Sugana, all of a sudden, said, "Brother, why don't you start for the village, as you had planned to?"

"Oh yes, I must go."

"It's a cloudy evening and darkness is spreading on all sides. Start immediately while there is still some light to avoid snakes and scorpions."

"We can be careful only when we see them and if people could live simply by being careful, who will die then? The village is only two miles away and won't take me very long to reach. Don't sleep in the low cot. Make sure that you raise it. Should it rain, spread some tarpaulin. Don't lie on the ground in the cottage lest there be snakes because of excessive sultriness."

"Agreed," said Sugana.

Sinath left, but darkness was deepening like collyrium because of the thick clouds. It was the fourth day of the waxing moon, the bright half of the lunar *'Bhadawa'*. The moon was up in the sky but was not bright enough to enable Sinath locate his path . However, since he was accustomed to the path his legs did not carry him astray. He might have walked a hundred yards when he saw a bullock-cart and heard its welcome ringing.

Sinath said, "Who is there?"

"I am Pithi, the Nayak. Aren't you Sinath?"

"Yes, I am."

"Come then. Climb unto the cart".

Both were almost of the same age.

"Oh no, I'll reach soon on foot," Sinath said. "Why should I unnecessarily strain this poor old bullock?"

"It is because of the darkness that I am offering you this lift. Let Baba Rathore help us! With him, it's all light. You have walked half the distance. Why not cover the remaining half with me? We are in no hurry. How does it matter if we reach a little late?"

Sinath could not say 'no'. He climbed unto the cart. There was more than a maund of green grass in the cart. Sinath was curious to know whether it was for personal use or for sale. Pithi said that it was for neither. Sinath could not understand anything. The cartman then explained, "I had borrowed about five hundred rupees from Dhanji against my crop. He will charge no interest from me and I'll charge nothing for the grass."

"Is all this in writing and duly signed?" Sinath asked.

"It stands mortgaged against one of my wife's ornaments."

"What rate of interest is he going to charge you?"

"I'm not sure but it won't be less than four per cent per month."

"Even if we take it at five per cent, then for five hundred rupees the interest adds up to Rs. 25. If you always bring back nearly a maund of grass, and if you sell it for two rupees every day, you earn sixty rupees per month."

"When I go to the Seth he sometimes gives me vegetables, tea- leaves, pieces of jaggery etc. You are intelligent and well- meaning, but he is simple-hearted and unsophisticated. And who knows when he might prove helpful to me?"

Sinath did not reply but mused, "This fool is like a sheep who is born to be fleeced. The rich man might be giving him jaggery worth four rupees and tea worth half of that but the poor man does not understand how the rich becomes richer and the poor poorer still. They take undue advantage of others' weaknesses and constraints. And what the rich man gives is paltry, since whatever grain, grass, leaves and the like the poor man collects from his field is sold to the rich who always pay much less than what others would do for the same stuff. The poor man has no idea that he alone will be the ultimate sufferer."

Sinath said aloud, "You could have got a better price had you sold your ornaments in the market."

"Had I gone to a goldsmith or a businessman, he would have purchased it for half or at the most three-quarters of its actual value. It's beyond my capacity to have another piece made. And even if it did become possible sometime, the strain would have been unbearable. And then, Sinath, you know, no wife will easily part with her ornaments. But then, why bother? How long can a lamb escape the butcher's knife? Those who mean to slit it open are merely looking for the right time and opportunity."

"You are right, but since we have been born, we must live it out, well or ill."

"What about your field?"

"It all depends on the rainfall. When it is good, we have enough food for a year, otherwise not even fodder for the animals."

Thus conversing they neared the boundary of the village. Dim lights were flickering here and there. Sinath said, "Brother, I must get down here, otherwise I will have to take the longer path." Sinath got off the cart and made his way home. His mother was waiting for him. Tired and angry, she shouted at him for being late.

Sinath explained that he got delayed talking to Pithi Nayak.

He then ate some curry and *khichri,* a preparation of rice and lentils boiled together, that his mother had cooked and strolled out of the house.

It was late; must have been about 10 o'clock. The moon had set a little while ago. The sky was overcast with clouds. In the north- eastern direction, lightning flashed intermittently. It must be within twenty miles from the village, Sinath thought to himself. At times there was a rumbling sound along with the peacock's *'may-awe'*, now and then, Sinath mused, "The rain god has left his abode and should reach us soon. Let me call on the ailing head priest. If he's still alive, I'll be able to meet him, or else I'll return, which will mean just a little more exercise."

On the eastern side of the village were the houses of the Brahmans and the Vaishyas. The northern side was inhabited by the Jats. On one end of the western side, lived the Harijans, numbering about twenty families in all. Most of them were Naiks and Meghwals. In their close neighbourhood, lived half-a-dozen families of cultivators and some families of servants. In between, here and there, lived barbers, carpenters and other castes. In one part of the southern corner lived the potters, and in the other part were the oilmen and watermen. A single house is of the kalals. In all there must be three-hundred-and-fifty houses of which about sixty-five were pucca houses, spread here and there and the rest were thatched ones or a mixture of both. The village had got electricity connection a couple of years ago. About thirty prosperous houses had electric connections. At half- a-dozen prominent corners of the village there were street lights also. The village had a cistern. There was a *patwari,* the village officer who maintained land records. There was an Ayurvedic dispensary, a Municipal House, a Middle School and a Post Office. A bus plied through the village once a day. More than ninety per cent of the villagers were farmers. Agriculture was their main source of sustenance.

Sinath thought that he should take the longer route to the priest's house since the shorter one was rather dark. He had walked half the distance when he saw the potter, Gango, in the light of a dim street lamp. It was very close to Dhanji, the village Seth's residence. Gango called out, "Aren't you Sinath?"

He said, "Yes."

"Out at this time?"

"I have to live the rest of my life in peace," Sinath chuckled. "I am going to the right place. Tell me whence you have come."

"What shall I tell you?"

"I heard that there was some manhandling in the village and the police had to be called."

The potter related the whole story, "I shall conceal nothing from you. I have just been to Dhanji's place and mortgaged some of my wife's and my brother's wife's precious ornaments for Rs. 800. I need the money to bribe the police and an additional hundred for my own post-mortem rites, as it were."

"What about food?" Sinath asked.

"That was weighed at the Seth's shop and given to me."

"It does not matter that you did not consult me, but at such a time you should not have ignored your own children. You should not have spent everything on the bribe. This idiotic plan of yours will crush you to pieces, so much so that you will not even recover in two years. Who gave you such an advice?"

"The headman of the village and Guman singh".

"One is gluttonous and corrupt and the other a drunkard."

"Tomorrow I have to go to the police station to give evidence."

"They will not take your evidence for nothing. They will behave like greedy members of a marriage-party."

"What else could I have done? Otherwise those rogues would have devoured me."

"Do you think that a policeman will stand guard for you? In the end they too will plead for a compromise, which we could have made ourselves with just half the money."

Sinath looked at Gango. Gango's face was overshadowed with worry and tension. Saying that they will meet again, Sinath moved away. He mused, "Dhanna is sure to have fabulous earnings whether one fights or compromises, whether it is famine or floods. Even at the time of a bumper crop, people have to knock at his door to be swindled."

Sinath hurried his pace. He thought that if his purpose was not served, he would return and try the next morning. But it occurred to him that no matter how late he might be, there was no wife to either extend a red carpet welcome or to take exception to his being so late. Finally, he reached the Ramdwara gate. The lamp outside was glimmering dimly. A few feet away from the gate, a woman in a white sari and a boy of about sixteen passed him by. The woman's face was covered. She was carrying a bundle in her hand and the boy had a small box with him.

Sinath went inside the gate and gently pushed at the door.

He heard someone say, "Who is there? Come by the main gate." The small gate was reserved for sadhus. When he reached the main gate, a sadhu in his seventies opened the door.

Sinath said gently, "How is Mahantji? I want to have his *'darshan'*.

"He is senseless and hardly opens his eyes. Every ten minutes or so, he speaks a word or two. In any case, is this the time to come to see him? Better go and sleep."

Sinath watched the door close on him. He did not want to begin an argument and turned back right away. He had hardly left when he decided to retrace his steps. He stood silently near the door. He was alert enough to bear the seth asking the sadhu who the man outside was. The sadhu replied that he did not know, for he had not asked.

"You should have asked him. Was he alone?"

"He must have been alone, for I saw no one else with him."

Silence reigned again. Sinath waited for a minute or two and then started walking. The whole village was asleep and there was no sound. Only the dogs, hardly in their senses, were fighting. Their barking was just audible from a distance.

In front of him a bitch jumped from a wall followed by half-a- dozen infatuated dogs, a couple of whom were lame. Many were growling. Passing through a gap in a hedge, they entered the square in front of a house. They were snapping and snarling at each other. The master of a house screamed, "Stop, you rascals! Won't you let me sleep even for a few minutes." It sounded as if he had struck one with a stick. The dog ran howling loudly into the street.

An old and rather feeble dog failed to climb the wall, but went on trying with little success. Sinath mused, "Will this dog make its father immortal by skirmishing in this manner? They all are so desperate to mate. They just won't leave her alone. Thank God that they copulate for only two months in a year. If, like men, they were to indulge in sex all the year round, they would have the entire neighbourhood hanging in mid-air in exasperation. And of themselves, hardly one would be left in one piece, and that too, if he were really lucky."

He returned home. Lying down on his cot without the bed-clothes, Sinath tried to sleep. But he could not get even a wink of sleep. He lay thinking, "That woman must have been Dhanji's sister Chanda, a child-widow. Whatever valuable articles she had brought from her in-laws are now with her brothers. She would be about forty-five now and the boy by her side must have been her nephew. She is not so unwise as to bring somebody else on such an occasion. The hypocritical saint with his bald pate strove hard all his life like an ox, amassed wealth and kept guard over it like a snake. When they approached him for a contribution for the school, he did not give a single pie. Saying that he was an anchorite, he freed himself from all such nuisances. His actions were such as to warrant his fall. She must be off with all his precious things in her possession. Sinath had often seen her at the Ramdwara. Her dhoti was all white and her skin was the colour of wheat. In her hand there used to be a rosary of holy basil. She used to be in the service of ascetics and always at the forefront of the religious discourses. Even though her face was covered, her movements and bearing revealed that the woman he had seen that night was none other than Chanda. Sinath tried hard to sleep, but could not. He mused, "The priest treats patients with medicines and also makes use of talisman-like devices. He must be about sixty. He has recently put on some weight and his left hand shakes a little. He trusts no one, not even his father. And who can be sexually righteous these days? Tulasi has said that in the Kaliyug, the ascetics' gaze remains fixed on money and mansion. How right was he! The inner wall of the Ramdwara has engravings like, 'We have tried all elixirs but the topmost is the name of the Almighty. The name of Rama is for all to chant, since it costs nothing. Listen to me, O Parvati, those who are libidinous are really unfortunate'. But upstairs there is a well-equipped room with a fan fitted. There is a gaudy carpet on the floor. There is a bedstead on it. The glasses and other decorative pieces are such that even an otherwise calm person would get sexually excited. An anchorite or two are nearly always there. Once he had a disciple from Marwar. He was on the right side of twenty. In a month or so he was unceremoniously discharged. Another who replaced him met the same fate. He believes in eating alone and not sharing victuals with others. His passion for women and money would not let him have any other diversion. Most of his meals were sent by the Seth. Somebody or the other from the village would gladly play host to occasional sadhus. Festivals meant a solid income to the Ramdwara. However stale and malodorous things might become, he would not part with any item. Chanda alone was allowed to sort out things. Let it be so, what has Sinath got to do with all this? The priest will reap what he has sown, Sinath will not wash dirty linen in public.

He changed his side to see if he could sleep. He tried to think of other things but he could not, like the insect returning to the same spot inspite of being repeatedly pushed aside. "Who is there with the priest—Dhanna or his brother Lalchand? It is just possible that they are picking out some precious documents or elixirs from the old man's horde. In case the head priest is conscious, all this must be in accordance with his wishes." Sinath mused, "My promissory note will certainly reach them. Let it, since my dealing has never been underhand. I owe him Rs. 200, but I am not in a position to pay him back instantly. In the morning, if in the presence of ten people, I am asked to take back the promissory note because of non-payment, it will be embarrassing to me. I might have to sell the bullock, but will my parents let me do that? They have no idea of the principal sum borrowed by me. If that is known, it will create a real fuss."

He changed sides again and his thoughts, too, turned the other way. He mused, "Times are such that if you have to help others, help only if you have some money to spare.

If you can save nothing, don't be so foolhardy that your munificence boomerangs on you. Why should you go out of your way to borrow money for some other person, and that, too, in writing?" With this argument with himself, he examined his actions from all sides. "What wrong have I done if I have helped a poor Brahman? He was a T.B. patient and also my childhood pal. To cap it all, his daughter was of a marriageable age. Five minutes before he died, he spoke slowly with tears in his eyes, 'You know that there is not cloth enough for my winding sheet. Please help to see her marriage through'. His eyes were full of tears and his voice was broken with sobs. He had kept looking at Sinath wistfully. Raising his hand weakly, he had asked his daughter to come forward. She had stood weeping at her father's bedside. Sinath mused, "I am a Jat and a son of the soil. Let me wait hopefully for a good crop. With blessings from mother-earth nothing can go wrong. Why am I being so timid?"

The night ended, but not his worries. He must have slept for not more than half-an-hour. A few fading stars were still twinkling in the early morning sky. On opening his eyes he noticed that the wounded and disappointed dogs were still barking. In the early hours of the morning their barking sounded out of place and inauspicious. Half-a-dozen dogs were sitting close to the main entrance to the village. Sinath screamed abuses at them from his bed, but to no purpose. Then he got up, and drove them away with a stick. He heard some woman say, "The head priest is no more. The funeral procession will soon proceed to the cremation ground." Sinath said to himself, "As God has willed. I shall contact the Seth in the noon. Nobody will take exception to my calling on him. But it will not be nice if he calls me later. "

2

Nobody knew when exactly at night the priest had expired, or what had caused his death. All this, only God knew or those who were with the priest; but the fact remains that he is no more. The entire village, even without the barber's announcement, knew of it minutes before sunrise and they all wanted to have his *'darshan'*.

After taking his bath Sinath was talking to his aunt regarding some family matters. After her husband's death she was in severe financial straits. After the birth of her first son she had suffered much. He would have been of Sinath's age but he had died when he was not even three years old. Some "lamia" is said to have devoured him. The suspect was a sixty-year-old female potter. She had a scattered growth of long hair on her chin and lip. She used to come on ceremonial occasions like Holi and Diwali and demand gifts. Women would hide themselves and their infants in some hut or inner room of their dwellings when they saw her coming. Sinath's aunt herself had told him once, "I had gone to the well to fetch water and your mother was tending a calf at the rear of the house. It was on the eve of 'Akshaya Tritiya', a very auspicious day when the old potter-woman came to take her due. The boy was sleeping in a cradle. She looked at him hard and then turned away. The boy did not survive that night. In the morning he was just a broken, faded flower!"

This did not however convince Sinath. How can a woman kill someone simply by her looks ? She must be seeing somebody or the other everyday. The villagers are not all dead. Only those ignorant of diseases talk such nonsense. He probed his aunt further but she could hardly explain anything to him. Superstition is certainly irrational. Had the alleged "lamia" been living, he would have gone to see her and asked her everything. But she was dead. In her last years, afflicted by disease and starvation, she had become blind. She had lost control of her bowels and bladder. All the children, the five or six that she had borne, died one after the other. Her house was in ruins. How could Sinath have arrived at a logical conclusion? The seed of his curiosity was deeply sown, waiting for the compassionate rain of knowledge.

Sinath had once asked his late maternal uncle all about fiendish women. His uncle was a dispassionate soul who kept much to himself. Truly, he was a saint. He had said, "O my son, there is nothing like a"lamia". It is but the evil eye of a person. When a woman hungers for a child and such desire overpowers her, only then does she harm some child. It is called the black eye and is somewhat like black-marketing. Your outlook must not be narrow and as far as possible you must not be close-fisted. Narrow-mindedness and small-heartedness are pernicious to both ascetics and house-holders." This advice was imprinted in Sinath's mind. The seed of enlightenment began to sprout from that very day.

The milk of the breasts, if retained inside may cause untold misery and debilitate the body. Hence Sinath had sucked at the breasts of both his mother and his aunt. He must have been breast-fed by them for about a year. He acknowledges the right of the mother over that of his aunt, but the aunt always treated him as dearly as her first child. "She has been suffering from malaria for three days," Sinath said. "The weeding is finished. Now if rain blesses us, I'll be glad. That will be my fulfilment."

"Darling, there is many a slip betwixt the cup and the lip. You can be sure only when the grain is stored in the barn. Mere rainfall will not do. There must be no adverse winds.

They should be pleasing, not stormy. So many factors contribute to the success of crops." The headpriest used to say, "Don't feel proud, O farmer, on seeing bumper crops. There is no success until and unless all obstacles are surmounted."

She stood up the moment she heard the blowing of a conch-shell.

"What happened?"

"Didn't you hear the sound of the conch-shell? Let me have a glimpse of the funeral procession."

"Here, let me support you lest you should fall."

"Oh no, just bring a piece of coconut kernel from my box."

His aunt went out slowly and stood near the gate. Sinath gave her the asked for kernel.

The sky was reverberating with the collective chanting, the drums, conch-shells and the like. They were chanting, "Ramdasji Maharaj ki jai". The procession moved along; the crowd swelling by degrees. Sinath too stood at a corner of a street.

The bier was gaudily decorated. Four men held it on their shoulders. The priest had been dressed in new clothes. His head was decked with a red turban of fine muslin. His shirt, too, was of muslin and his spectacles had been placed on his nose. There was a small round mark of vermilion and sandal-paste on his forehead. He looked splendid, propped up in his wooden seat. In his hand was placed a thick garland of beads of fresh basil. At his back was a calendar of Rama and Sita . In the front stand was placed a copy of the Ramayan published by the Gita Press, Gorakhpur. In the incensory aloes were glittering. The atmosphere was quite aromatic. A piece of wood, the size of a hand, was placed under his chin to support his head. Women and children followed the bier. In the front, were about fifty people, all eager to lend a shoulder to carry the body. Each one was awaiting his turn. Such was the religious fervour to be a coffin-bearer.

Women came out to have a glimpse of the priest. Some were standing on the roofs and many young wives were peeping round the corner of their veils. People were offering coconuts, copra and *batashas.* Dhanji was throwing fistful of small coins which were being picked up by the Nayaka, Meghwal, and Sansi children. Some women were heard saying that the dead priest looked much more handsome than when alive.

Sinath gazed at the corpse of the priest for a couple of minutes and then at the women standing around. Sinath noticed a domineering-looking woman among the crowd and recognised Chandabai. The procession marched forward but Sinath stayed where he was for quite some time. He was stirred deeply and lost in thought.

"How gaudily was the corpse decorated," mused Sinath, "even more than the living body!" The priest was a hypocrite. Even his corpse was bespectacled. What was he to see now? Even when alive he saw very little. Right from his youth, he had started wearing dark glasses. On the walls of his room were engraved sayings like, 'The name of Rama is for all to take', but he did not seem to have ever seen the writing on the wall. He, who enjoyed the bliss of being served by all and sundry and earned a name for himself, was a servant of passion and money and that too, at his own Ramdwara. A shield and a sword always hung from his waist. He was replete with evil propensities and yet the world worshipped this repository of sin!

"I gave him a promissory note for Rs. 200 and said, 'Your honour, the poor woman has hardly anything, not even enough for a square meal. I will repay the money to you, but be kind enough to reduce the rate of interest in this case'. His reply was typical. He said 'Sinath, my rate of interest for others is Rs. 4, even 5, but from you I will charge just two per cent per mensem!' I had nothing to say.

The priest had no one and was thus unable to appreciate the difficulties of others. Any kind of help was out of question. He could not even forgo the interest on the principal sum." Sinath had been so angry that he felt like slapping him . He was so disgusted that he shunned his company for quite sometime. But then, a dead body is beyond all hatred. It is free from all emotional bonds. As such he ought to overcome his resentment.

He now recalled Nathli Darogi. She had swept the Ramdwara for twenty years. She cleaned the utensils and washed the clothes. Rarely was she given any thing in return. All day long she chanted the name of Rama and talked pleasantly to all.Her hut was made of mud. Once when the rain had devastated it, she begged the priest, "Guru Maharaj, where shall I put my flour? The dogs and cats will spoil it."

But the priest was made of sterner mettle. He said, "Why don't you weave some 'Kheep' (a leafless plant with long and thin strands). Smear them with a little dung and clay, leaving some spaces in between. The wickers will thus get fixed and last for years. How long have you to live that you should think of making a pukka house?"

Sinath mused, "Yes, she may have lived for a few more years but for the priest". The poor woman had appealed to Chanda, but she paid little heed to her pleading. The ugly and the beautiful were all alike. Chanda is, after all, the priest's disciple. Nathali died, otherwise she would have seen the departing priest who had a bungalow of his own. While doing his cot and bed, he must have taken with him a heavy load of sins and crimes. Nathali lived her short life smilingly in her cottage and then one day she was found dead. For several years she had maintained herself by working in several houses. There was once some talk of her having stolen some valuables.

Another woman belonging to a goldsmith family came his way accidentally. She died three years back.

Two years ago Agaria Vaishya mortgaged ornaments weighing twenty tolas against Rs. 5000 at the rate of three rupees per hundred. He could not pay interest for three months and was summoned. He went there with two of his friends. Sinath, too, was there. Agaria said, "Here is your money with interest. Now please let me have my ornaments."

The priest took out the bundle. Agaria looked at it suspiciously and said, "What shall I do with these? I want the ones I gave you."

The priest's face turned pale. He said, "Whom do these belong to if not to you?"

"How am I expected to know that? Thousands of people come to you. I know for certain that these are not mine".

"No, these are yours. I do not lie."

"If you do not lie, I, too, have sworn to be truthful. Keep these ornaments with you. In case you have forgotten, please try to remember things." Agaria stood up to leave and said, "They belong to my daughter who will go to her in-laws tomorrow. So please hurry up and find the right ones."

The priest's heart missed a beat. He called his goldsmith and showed the ornaments to him. The goldsmith said, "The cost of these is not more than ten rupees. They are just polished brass." The priest nearly died.

He used to go out to treat patients but the fee was his first consideration. To begin with, it was just a rupee; later he doubled it. Even when he saw a patient dead, he did charge his fee. But the money that he amassed had little to do with these fees. His real money-spinners were his so-called magical potions. He had recipes for birth-control. Widows and women from barber, carpenter and goldsmith families approached him in confidence. Many of his disciples were, in fact, simply his touts. Similarly, he prescribed talismans for the birth of sons. He was a fake physician. If his talisman worked by chance, he would receive offerings, yearly services and other presents. If it failed, even then he was a gainer, for the cost of the talisman, a single paisa, easily fetched twenty-five rupees. He was adept at getting a poor man's fields for half their price; also their cows, sheep, buffaloes and camels.

Sinath wondered how such a man had verses like, 'Listen, O Uma! Unfortunate are they who discard God and indulge in indiscriminate sex' written and put up on his walls. The priest himself was such an unfortunate person. He did not hate his own sins, but only gazed upwards! Behind the cursed corpse, there was the Sitaram calendar, assuring him of safety and protection. While living, he must not have used his prayer beads even for a few minutes. Now in his dead hands there was a peacock-feather and in front of him, the Ramayan. His arms were covered with sandal- paste. So were his fingers, chest and navel. Some lucky woman's fingers must have been imprinted there. Was this the way of becoming a Tulasidas? Now will follow the other formalities. His cremation will need ghee, sandal-paste, copra and what not. Then the seat on his tomb and footprints thereon. Also dates of birth and death and all the glowing words. They will make this mud worm a historic saint!

There will be a general feast especially for the mendicants. Offerings will be made to the guest priests. Some successor will be appointed. The priest must have nominated his successor before his death. The new man may even outdo his predecessor. Such unholy souls spoil everything. Their lasciviousness and greed will render them unfit to hold this office. But who can say these things to those who stand around enamoured of corpses. They feel gratified carrying such corpses. Let this be over, for there is no end to such tales. Irritated, he stood up and made up his mind to contact Dhanna Seth in the afternoon.

It was about 10.30 A.M. As soon as he finished his meal, he saw Tikku goldsmith. He was a pleasant fellow, in his early thirties. He had a ready stock of all kinds of neighbourhood gossip. People called him the 'Narada' of the village. His vocation was one of no profit and no loss, which provided for his needs. Story-telling was a side-business which kept him busy.

Sinath said, "Come on, Tikku I heard that you arrived last night. Tell me something about the village."

"What I have heard today has simply flabbergasted me."

"What's it? I don't follow you."

"Two sadhus, with a woman and a child have arrived by the morning bus. They are young and the woman with them is slightly older. The boy is about twelve. I accompanied them to Ramdwara. The woman seemed to be of the barber caste and had been there once or twice earlier. 'Let God protect us. It seems that you have missed the last 'darshan' of the head-priest,' I said to her.

'Yes, it's a matter of chance,' she replied. 'You must have received a letter,' I said.

"Who would inform me? A passerby told me of it. I know why no letter was sent to me. His clever disciple has bungled everything. I am not going to be outwitted by her, since I know about the smallest of ornaments in the house. My name is Pema. I have endured many hardships in my life. You may change my name if I fail to secure everything back,' she said.

'Things here seem to be in the care of Chandabai,' I said.

'Yes, I know all that. She has been changing sides. I know the secrets even of the Seth,' she said.

I looked at her face intently for a couple of minutes. That she is the craftiest and most worldly-wise woman was written on her face. Resuming the conversation I said, 'Some disciple of his will succeed him and it is for him to take care of the entire stock.'

Placing her hand on the boy, she said excitedly, 'He is the true successor.'

'How is that, Madam?' I asked her.

'It is because he is his son and I am his wife.'"

"God protect us," Sinath interjected, "but wasn't he a renouncer?"

"Can't householders be renouncers? He studied to be a physician and always repeated the name of God. Is earning money sinful?"

'If I am not mistaken, some forty years ago, you had wedded Ramswaroop.'

'He was this boy's father,' said Pema.

'Had he then only one child?'

'He had also a daughter whose hand was given to a man at Nagaur, Mandore. The daughter and son-in-law will both be coming here in about three days.'

"God protect us! Had he no more children?" Sinath asked.

"Some eleven years ago he felt himself detached from the world and left his family."

"God help us! What if this boy who is to succeed marries later?"

"He knows it best. How can we foresee his future? If he should be unable to lead an ascetic life, he may marry, which is equally good."

"And what if he is not named the successor?"

'I will then go on a hunger-strike and kill myself. But who can prevent his investiture? What woman has eaten dry ginger with pure ghee and has the courage to oppose me?'

'With God's help, Madam, all praise to you, as also to your parents and husband. Your resolve has strengthened my belief in you. I'm the yellow ochre of your feet. This I want to put on my forehead. I will certainly help you.'

This pleased the woman very much and she smiled a little. Sinath said, "You have outdone the police officer in recording statements. Weren't those two sadhus there?"

"Of course, they were watching us intently, and listened to all we talked about. They must have taken me to be the most reliable person in the village. I stood up and then one of them followed me and said, 'The real successor is inside. He is a saint. I have merely accompanied him. Till date, he has treated patients suffering from all kinds of diseases including venereal ones. This woman is an impostor and is out to grab more property. Earlier too she had decamped with goods worth Rs. 3000. Till date she has treated patients suffering from venereal diseases not unlike Ramdasji. Thus having gained his favour, Tikku was to go home.'

"Tikku, it is clear that the whole thing is in a mess," said Sinath.

"If not all, at least some part of it is."

"Let it end in smoke. The very foundation of Ramdwara was laid at an inauspicious hour."

Tikku said, "Your reference to the foundation reminds me of another thing."

"Tell me ."

"My grandpa used to say that the grandfather of Ramdas was a *sorcerer* and trickster. He was the first to come here. A young Chaudhari woman used to visit the Ramdwara now and then. She was a good-looking, simple and virtuous wife. One day the priest, overwrought with passion, gave her a sugar-candy as prasad, before she left for home. The priest said, 'This is from the offerings made to the idol. Eat it on reaching home. God helps the needy.' Unfortunately the candy got crushed against the door-frame and was broken into pieces. She thought howsoever sacred it might be, it was not worth eating. Collecting all its pieces, she dropped them into the buffalo's feed. That evening, after eating its food, the buffalo started lowing in an odd way. The Chaudhari could not make out any thing. Since the buffalo had given birth to a calf the other day, there could be no question of her being in "heat". The Chaudhari gave her one of his usually effective home remedies, but it did not help. He untied her from the stake to see if that would help, but the moment she was freed, she ran away and stood in front of the Ramdwara's cell. The Chaudhari brought it back with a lot of difficulty, and locked it up. Even then it did not calm down. He had enough experience of what villagers did in such cases. He rightly suspected some fly in the ointment. He asked his wife, "What did you give the buffalo to eat today?"

She said, "Nothing but the usual feed."

"Was there nothing out of the usual in it?"

After thinking for a while she said, "Yes, I did throw some pieces of a sugar-candy into the feed."

"Where did you get it from?" he asked her.

" Baba gave it to me. He asked me to eat it at home, but since it was broken, I dropped it into the feed for our buffalo."

The Chaudhari understood all and let the buffalo out. It charged towards the Baba's cottage. He followed it and called the Baba out. The Baba called out to ask who it was.

The Chaudhari said, "Madam is waiting outside and is on pins and needles to have darshan. Better come out and welcome her."

When the Baba came out, the Chaudhari struck him several blows. He asked him how long he had been distributing sugar-candies. The Baba fell at the Jat's feet and begged his forgiveness. He assured him that no harm would come to the buffalo and that he would heal it. When the buffalo became normal, the Jat brought it home. The Baba had been taught a lesson and the woman decided never to visit the Baba's abode again."

Sinath listened to Tikku and said, "This is nothing but a cock- and-bull story."

"Think what you please; but this is what I had heard from my grandpa. And what do I gain by telling a lie? I have merely repeated it, and that too without appropriating anything as goldsmiths proverbially do."

"Whatever be the case, the fact is that a sensuous person in the garb of a sadhu is simply detestable".

"That's right, but I am getting late and feeling awfully hungry."

"Go then."

Tikku moved away and Sinath lay for a while.

3

Sinath's mother said, "I had sent for aromatic seeds from Seth Hajarimal and what he has given is all chaff."

"Shall I get you some from Dhanji, if he should have the right stuff?"

"He is no better. They are all chips of the same block. I have to give a mixture of it boiled in ghee and jaggery to my daughter- in-law."

Sinath placed the seeds in his palm, smelt them and folded back the small paper packet. "Such seeds should not even be given away in charity," said Sinath and went out.

On his way, he met Raju Meghwal and his teen-aged daughter, who was accompanying him. Sinath asked, "What's wrong with you?"

"Sir, I am going to Hazarimal. My daughter had gone there with two loads of dry wood which must have been a little more than a maund. In exchange he gave her this half-seer of jaggery and this small packet of tea, hardly sufficient even for a single cup. See for yourself if I am exaggerating."

Sinath said that he too was going there.

There were four houses in that street. They all belonged to the Oswals. The street was all muddy and presented a repelling sight. The mud was an awful mixture of dirty rags, gobs of spit, pieces of paper, dogs' excreta and urine. None passing that way could afford to breathe.

"Raju, come carefully. Don't get stuck in the mire," Sinath said. "Since the pipe-lines have been installed in houses, it has become all muddy here."

Sinath said, "These people have tried to protect religion so much that they will not even let flies and mosquitoes die. What would they lose if they learnt to live hygienically? But who can awaken the already awakened? What daring person can ever challenge them?"

"Your honour, it's a dangerous task to pass this way in the dark, but we fear to talk to the people of influence about this, and if we do not, life becomes unbearably hard. In case our feet get stuck in this mud, no one will even offer water to wash them."

"Why should you unncessarily strain your throats asking for water to wash? Simply rub sand onto it and it will dry in no time."

"But where is the sand in this God-forsaken street?"

"That is true indeed."

Thus talking, they reached the shop. The Seth was seated in a corner of the verandah. Near at hand lay a fly-swat. In front of him there was a sun-dial. On a raised seat there was a veil and the Seth sat bare-bodied. On the northern side, very close to the verandah there was a windmill. Most of the low-caste people, whether local or outsiders, purchased cereals from here and also got their grain ground. In the rainy season most of the villagers thronged there for their daily needs. All domestic grinding mills lay idle for four months and it was only then that the womenfolk became comparatively free. One had to put up with foreign matter in the flour. These days who complains when things are stale and sour? If what should be saffron-coloured millet turns out to be black--if what should be fine quality wheat turns out to be coarse, how does it matter when you want to enjoy some leisure ? On the northern side of the verandah, there was a tailor's shop, so tiny that it could accommodate but one person. Both the shops belonged to the Seth. His grandson was in charge of the windmill.The Seth earned rent from the tailor, and also got all his clothes stitched free of cost.

Sinath and Raju entered the shop. Nathmal, the Seth's son, as also his fifteen-year-old son were busy weighing things. At the rear there was a gate for entry and exit. The back portion was very spacious. There was an iron gate through which a truck could pass. The gate was now open. There was a big heap of wood and tree-trunks. There was another heap beside it. On one side there was a balance. In one of the pans of the balance there were weights and stones. There were about ten women sitting around, whose stock of wood had just been weighed. They were waiting for payment to enable them purchase their necessities from the shop.

Nathmal said, "Welcome, Sinath! What brings you here today?"

"I have just come by. There is nothing special. Deal with these women first, and then we will talk at leisure."

The women were from Nayak and Meghwal families. A couple of them seemed to be pregnant. They remained standing for a few minutes and then sat on one side. Two dry tree-trunks had been weighed and settled for at the rate of Rs 1.75 per maund. Women of the family or even one of the children, would go to the jungle and collect the wood at one place and then skilfully arrange them in a neat bundle, which they then brought to the Seth from a distance of no less than three miles. Some of them carried loads of no less than thirty kilograms. In a single family if there were two or three persons to carry such loads, they could manage with comparative ease.

The married daughter of the Kotwal said, "Your Honour, Hema's wife has to hurry because she has to breast-feed her child, left alone at home."

Nathmal said, "Have a little patience. We are not running away from here."

Another woman said, "I left home after a meagre breakfast before sunrise. I shall have to cook the food on reaching home. I had planned to purchase millet, but if I take it now, when will it be ground and kneaded? So I will have to buy flour from the windmill."

The Kotwal's daughter said, "The flour is often adulterated, my dear sister-in-law! Don't purchase it without tasting. Nobody will take back your kneaded flour." From what she said it was clear that she herself had had such experience.

Another one said, "Nathmalji, last night I had taken a couple of table-spoonfuls of mash that has caused diarrhoea. Even now I am feeling restless."

Nathmal said, "I too have taken nothing but my morning-tea. Father takes food just once in three days. Think of him and you...."

Sinath asked whether his father would abstain from food altogether for three days.

"No food at all," he replied. "He will take only a few drops of lime juice in warm water."

"What he does is really marvellous."

The Kotwal's daughter said, "Without work there is no food for us. Without food it is impossible to work."

Another young woman commented, "We could also fast for three days, but our children cannot do without their mothers' milk. And milk can be had only when blood courses through the veins. All this requires food."

Still another one said, "How long can the hungry dig stubs ? Just try and see it yourself."

Nathmal said, "To observe religious rites is no child's play."

Sinath was listening to their conversation. The stench of the foul mud hung in the air. He said, "It takes no effort to generate mud, but one cannot work hard without effort. I am at a loss to understand what makes for religion and what for the reverse."

Nathmal said, "Religion is the sharp edge of a sword. Not any and every body can practise it."

Sinath said, "These people dig stumps from the grcund and so insects are bound to be crushed."

"Yes, you are right."

"But tree stumps and us human beings are born together. When the tree stumps are taken out by digging the earth, insects will certainly die. And no digging, no stumps. Thus incurs sin."

"I cannot say I entirely agree with you, but let us end the argument. However, since the income from it is mostly yours, a good part of the sin must be shared by you."

Raju said, "Sinath, who can vie with them? They roll in wealth. Their birth is the result of their meritorious deeds. They are charitable. They nourish the hungry. They give something or other to a policeman, Patwari, village-sewak, and clerk, according to their means. The poor always give them some trouble or the other."

Sinath laughed and said, "You are a Kotwal. These things are too deep for you. Mere superficial study won't do."

Before Sinath could complete his statement, the Kotwal's daughter said, "Sinath, enough of your babbling. It's beyond our comprehension. First let us be paid. We are exhausted and the children at home are crying. You better indulge in your talk later. There will be time enough for that."

Nathmal said, "Rattu, here is your payment of one rupee and twelve annas. Rookhari, here is two rupees for you. The two bundles of grain that your two children bought have also been paid for."

Rattu said, "How is it, sir, that Rookhari has been paid two rupees and I four annas less? What I brought is heavier than hers."

"Yours must have been a little wet. Hence four annas must rightly have been deducted. I can give only what is recorded against each name."

"We both picked up our two bundles from the very same spot. Why then such highhandedness ?"

"Girl, your dues and her dues must have been mixed up in the record. Take ten paise more and cheer up. The difference we will make up sometime in some other way."

"Four stubs were taken as weighed without actually being weighed by you. You have thus paid me fifteen paise less."

Having said this the girl turned towards the windmill. Most of them were to take flour from there, though some took tea and jaggery.

Nathmal said, "What do I earn? My job is to put this into one pan and that into the other pan. But sitting idle is no less irksome. I have to deal with these people very tactfully. I earn just four to six annas wages per maund as my share."

In the meantime, a Brahman boy of about sixteen reached the shop. "Yes, what can I do for you?" Nathmal asked. He had come to collect Rs 90, the pay-off to the Patwari. The Seth gave him the money and the boy went off.

Sinath held out the aromatic seeds in the palm of his hand. "Just see here. Even four times this weight would make no difference, since it is all chaff."

The Seth looked at Sinath and then said to the boy, "Who gave this?" The boy said that he did not know.

"If you do not know, has some outsider come and sold this? Pay some attention to the customers you are dealing with."

The Seth took the seeds back from Sinath and emptied them into an old Dalda tin. He gave Sinath the right stuff of equal weight.

Sinath said, "Now, Seth, listen to this Rajia who seems to be bubbling with complaints." The Seth did not really like Sinath and feared him a little.

The Seth said to the Kotwal, "I do not know who gave you this. Take this pinch of tea and a piece of superfine jaggery that would be eminently suitable for a newly born son's mother. You are our Kotwal and you alone are ever ready to help us even at midnight."

The Kotwal assured the Seth that he was always at his beck and call. The Seth asked him to put some pieces of wood on one of the projecting shelves. The Kotwal and his daughter went outside to do the task. Sinath mused, "What a recompense for his tale of woe! This little bit of jaggery and tea will cost him dear. The poor man's eyes will shrink, since both he and his daughter will have to labour for at least an hour-and-a-half. The question of paying the poor man for his services was unlikely. The Seth, however, is adept at such things. But how can we prevent their exploitation when they themselves do not realize their plight? When they have agreed to work, who am I to forbid them?"

Sinath got up. On the right side above the almirah there hung a photo of 'Navkar' (Sacred to Jains). Noting his interest in the picture, the Seth said, "It's hardly a month since it was hung." Sinath said that was why he had never seen it before. Leaving the shop, he came out on the verandah. Nathmal bolted the door from inside. Seth Hazarimal was not in his meditative posture, which meant he must have been inside. In a corner, a dog suffering from scabies and besmeared with mud was sleeping care free.

Sinath waited for a minute or two near the stairs. He knew that walking through the mire was more arduous than crossing the Styx. He remembered the frank statement of the Kotwal's daughter, "Enough of your babbling. We understand it not. We are dying and the children are crying at home," she had said. The girl's lips were encrusted. Her face was shrivelled. Her acute hunger was reflected in her eyes. Such must be the plight of the other women as well. The intestines of the pregnant ones must be shrinking inside. Since there was no milk in their mothers' breasts, children would not stop crying. Only when there is water in a tank, can one get it through a pipe. But the children still continued sucking at the dry breasts. They are born poor and hungry, but who cares to discover its root? Whatever loaves they bake, whether properly heated or not, will serve as food for the old people in fields. They do not even have enough salt and pepper. They force their victuals down with water. They spend their life in great distress. They are always half-fed and half- clad. If they were to be told of some hunger-strike lasting for days or of the niceties of non-violence, it would be Greek and Latin to them. How can people who are famished assimilate such nonsense? They have to make ready pans, trenches, huts, ploughs and all that. Even after working very hard, they may hope to just about subsist. The girl had rightly said, "Your philosophy is beyond our comprehension."

The sleeping dog suddenly lifted its head and pricked up its ears. Sinath was startled. His chain of thought snapped. As he walked, some drops of muddy water soiled his clothes. The shirt would have to be washed at home. He could not help abusing and cursing the Seth. He met the Brahman boy on the way. On his shoulder was a tin which could contain about six kilograms of flour. Sinath said to him, "Boy, isn't grain ground at home these days?"

"It belongs to the Patwari," was the reply.

"How much is it?"

"Five kilos."

"What has he given you to do this?"

"Nothing."

"Why not?"

"He never gives anything. Nor does the village Sewak. I often do the job for both of them."

"So they give you nothing at all?"

"Bare thanks. However, if I am late for school some days, they ask the teachers not to scold me."

Sinath walked with him for quite some distance. He mused, "When these fellows pay him nothing for carrying the pounded grain, there is no question of the Sarpanch and Secretary paying anything. They do not lag behind in exploiting the poor, and thus make money. The Seth can have no one else so cheap. He must not be paying more than five rupees each to his four employees. Even a hare will cost more. Nathmal deserves all kudos."

Sinath asked him where he could find the Patwari. The boy said that he was in the Panchayat House.

"What is he there for?"

"Many animals were auctioned at a cattle pound. He must be accounting for them."

"Who else is there?"

"The Sarpanch, the village Sewak, the Patwari and the Secretary are all there."

"Do you know what has been auctioned recently?"

"A heifer, a cow and an old she-camel."

"Can you recall what the heifer went for?"

"The Kotwal had bid sixty rupees for it, but it was meant for Hazarimal." The boy took another lane. Sinath mused over it. "The boy has spoken the truth. Just sometime back he took ninety rupees from the Seth. One bottle of wine each was meant for the Patwari and Secretary; the balance for the Sarpanch and Village Sewak, including a fiver for the Kotwal. This had ensured that the heifer would come to the Seth's yard. The simple-hearted Raju Kotwal had said, 'They are sons of the goddess of wealth. They feed the Patwari, the village Sewak and the others.' He does not know that the fruit of labour never goes to the cultivator. The cream is dexterously snatched by the capitalist.

Sinath had often seen the heifer at the cattle pound. It was from Sind and was about three years old. Gifted with a beautiful pair of horns, she was very gentle and seemed to be pregnant. In case she delivered a calf in about six months, she would be worth two thousand rupees. She would look so charming that none would part with her even for two thousand. At the very first birth the yield of her milk will be not less than 5 kilograms. Some holy soul will milk her; but the girl had hit the point when she said, 'No philosophizing when we lie dying'. No one can do without food. Clothing and a roof are the next requisites. Religion can be thought of only when these three minimum necessities are well taken care of.

Sinath reached home, worried that he had taken so long to take the aromatic seeds back to his mother.

4

Seth Dhanji's shop was large and the building was 'pukka'. It was a general store. Salt, oil, tobacco, and all daily necessities were available there. He even kept pearls and coral. Lip-stick, nail polish and some other cosmetics were well displayed in the front almirah. It did not matter if the purchasers were mostly girls from Nayak, Sansi and Meghwal families; also their young, glittering wives. The shopkeeper must earn money irrespective of the breed of the purchaser. A priest must have his fee, whether the bride dies or the bridegroom.

On the round pillars of stone stood a big verandah for the convenience of the purchasers. Looking out on it was a large iron window, behind which was the house inside. A little more than two decades ago it was a desolate place. Owls used to hoot frighteningly in dark of night. Even during the day, no one felt really at ease. There were two trees, one a khajari and the other a big old tree which was the home to iguanas and owls. Birds had built their nests in it and bees their hives.

A junk-dealer had a small room where the shop stood today. This portion and the other half were used as a bedroom. A lantern used to give a dim light till 10 P.M. In that very dim light the Seth used to do his accounting.

Now the goddess of wealth had showered her blessing on him. In what used to be that very desolate place shone forth the smiling house with a basement. On the side of the house there were two plots of agricultural land. The Seth had bought a tractor some two years ago. In the spring season. It worked near the gutter. In the months of 'Ashadh' and 'Sawan'. It was given out on rent. There was thus no limit to his profit. He was thinking of buying a truck in six months. Milk, curd and butter were in abundance. In the yard there was a cutting machine which was used not only by the local people but also by the people of the neighbouring villages. He employed a farmer to do his agriculture and another person to pat the dung into cakes. He had a boy at the shop who worked at the weighing-balance.

The Seth had two brothers. Two of their children were studying at Bikaner. With the expanding family their business was flourishing. Both brothers earned lots of money by whatever means possible. Even in a jungle, they would have been capable of making money, the only condition being that there must be people to deal with. No official or clerk of the court could do without having something to do with them. Their reputation was high and income higher still. In the village there was a temple. Pandit Ramdas served there and also visited the shop for half an hour to recite 'Gopal Sahasranam'.

It must have been about half past eleven in the forenoon. After the priest's funeral rites, Dhanna Seth was just back at the shop. His bald pate, shining spectacles and the round sandal paste mark on his forehead gave him the appearance of one of great spiritual learning. He wore a thin rosary of 'rudraksha' (the seeds of the tree *cleocarpus ganitrus*) as advised by a sadhu who had assured him that it would ward off high blood- pressure. The Seth was in his early fifties. He had his cash-box in front of him. Girdhari, a Brahman boy in his twenties was in charge of the work of weighing. The Seth himself talked to the customers, asked about their requirements and received payments. The Seth had taken his pen out and was drawing lines in his account book with meticulous care. After drawing four lines, he hung the pen over his ear as though it were a pen-stand. When he raised his eyes he saw the barber Karna standing before him.

As soon as he stepped into the shop, the Seth said, "How have you come?"

"I have come on foot, but you know that nobody comes to you without some purpose."

"What do you want?"

"I need twelve hundred rupees."

"Such a big sum can be had only from the bank. Tell me what you need it for."

"You are our bank. My son's marriage has been fixed."

"Aren't marriages prohibited in the rainy season?".

"My idea was that, with God's grace, the crop would be good. I would have performed the marriage in summer quite easily, but, your Honour, man proposes and God disposes. I have had to incur some heavy expenses, quite uninvited and unasked for. My son's would-be-grand-father-in-law expired. My son's would-be-father-in-law came to see me himself. Putting his hand against his chin, he said to me, 'Master, I will offer saffron and my daughter and similarly you need not spend anything, not even on a leaf of myrtle'. While leaving, he also said that on the same date his granddaughter Pemli would also be a bride in a group-marriage. Please tell me with what face I could have said 'no' to him. In our community there is a great virtue in giving away a daughter in marriage."

"So you yielded for your good, since Laxmi is to knock at your door. She will massage her mother-in-law's feet and serve hot cakes to you."

"Yes, the times are such for people like you and not for the poor like me. In our case, if we are not beaten in our old age we would be as thankful as if we had been served hot cakes."

"So, on what terms do you want the money?"

"I have about ten sacks of grain and lentils."

"Are they clean and free of gravel?"

"Perfectly clean. No gravel, no small parts of the plant either."

"They must not be too thin. They should be such that they become soft in water."

"You must have no doubts, sir. Can there be knots in the yarn spun by a Muslim woman? You are welcome to check each grain."

"Tell me the rate."

"Who can hide the stomach from a midwife? The report is that the market rate is Rs. 1.25."

"Let's make it Rs. 1.15; and look here, I will get it weighed."

The Seth watched the barber's face intently. He mused, "The barber has come to me in his dire need. The goddess of wealth has sent him here to suffer loss which, however, is my gain. I must therefore tackle him as best as I can." He said to the barber, "If you take it elsewhere, say to the town 25 miles away, you will have to pay cartage. Then brokerage, octroi, and the wholesale market taxes would also have to be paid. It will mean two days of work there during which time you will have little time for food or even for a bath. No wise villager would ever think of selling his stuff in the town. If you want to invite trouble, go by all means and see if I am not correct."

The Seth's words softened the barber's attitude. He said, "I will have to manage a house to take the bridegroom around. When will I go to the city? When will I bring sisters and daughters home?"

He said to the Seth, "Please see to it yourself. My loss will be your gain, since it will not go to any third party. Will you be pleased to consider my case a little favourably?"

"How can I allow myself to undergo such a great loss? Afterall, I too have to live. The rate must be the same for all."

"Even then, do listen to me please."

"See, I meant to purchase at the rate of one rupee per kilo. Had somebody else been in your place, that would have been my offer. It's just for your sake that I am paying a little extra. Empty your sacks and take the money. You must have seen the auspicious bird on your right side. You are lucky!"

"Then I will bring it," said the barber and left.

When the Seth went out onto the verandah, he saw a woman shrunk into her mantle. A girl, not very young, was sitting close to her. The Seth asked her the purpose of her visit. The old woman adjusted her mantle and stood up. Her body was wrinkled all through. Her skirt from waist to ankle was torn and patched here and there. She was also shaking a little.

The Seth said, "Mother! speak out." Adjusting her mantle once again, she spoke slowly, "Your Honour, my daughter is to go to her in-laws. My son-in-law is at home to take her. I cannot send her without some gifts, but I have nothing with me. She herself had brought about 5 kilograms of gum secretly from Banwalia, at her father-in-law's house. She is a good, deserving girl. I must see her off with grace to maintain our pride." She stopped for a minute because of a fit of asthmatic coughing and then continued, "My old husband has gone out. Please give me some money. A blind man and an ignorant person are both alike. I know this much that she is the daughter of the village and that you are her parent- like protector."

So saying, she lay down again.

"Are you running a temperature?" the Seth asked.

The girl said, "It is malaria."

"These days it is an epidemic. Let me see your gum." The girl placed the pouch before him. The gum was excellent. The Seth knew the market rate, since he had purchased half a kilo at the rate of sixteen rupees ten days back. He used to eat a preparation made out of gum as a tonic every morning. The gum was weighed. It was 50 grams less than five kilograms. The Seth said, "Fifty grams makes no difference. She is our own. Here is Rs. 35." The old woman summoned up all her strength to say, "This is hardly sufficient for our needs, which are a mantle, a blouse and a skirt." A daughter is cared for by the mother alone. Sufficient or insufficient. It will help a little if you have such a liking for her."

The Seth handed over thirty-two rupees, saying that he had still to give a balance of three rupees.

"You have gratified us indeed. May you live for ages! We subsist under your shade. Now please give us rice and jaggery worth three rupees." In addition, the Seth gave the old woman two quinine tablets asking her to take them with tea to be rid of her fever. She blessed him. Leaning heavily on her daughter, she hobbled away.

The Seth had been clever enough to snatch both money and blessing. It was his profit and their pleasure. Having settled the bargain, he went inside where his younger brother Lalchand was sitting.

"When did you come?"

"I have just arrived."

"What about market-rates?"

"The wholesale rate of lentils in the city is Rs 1.60, ghee 34, millet 1.30 and that of the others remains unchanged. I have taken a truck-load of wheat at the rate of Rs. 1.15. At that rate it is a gift. It will be delivered to us from Anupgarh by day-after-tomorrow. Have you received some items here?"

"About twenty sacks of lentils at the rate of Rs. 1.05; two tins of ghee at the rate of 18.50; about ten sacks of millet at the rate of 1.05 and I have settled for 'gawar'. All that you get loaded in a truck. Also about six boxes of tea. Business in tea is profitable these days."

"That's right, because everyone drinks tea. Saints and prostitutes — all take a sip of tea."

"We stand to gain by its increasing use. Earlier we could sell half-a-box with difficulty. Now two boxes are sold with no effort at all and the demand is increasing daily."

"The priest passed away yesterday. For about three hours he could not speak a word. He breathed his last at about 3 A.M. Chanda and myself were present when he died."

Just then came Lalchand's son, Kanhaiyalal. He touched his grandfather's feet and remained standing.

"Have you just come with Lala?" the Seth asked.

"Yes."

"How long will your studies last?"

"About six more months."

"Then you will be a law graduate?"

"Yes, grandpa."

"Dear Kannu, manipulate things in such a way that you are appointed a magistrate. This will make me happy indeed. Even if you have to spend about five thousand rupees, it does not matter because money comes and goes."

"Baba, there is not the ghost of a chance, since there are a hundred candidates for a single post. People are prepared to pay an advance of thirty thousand rupees, and that too through some influential source."

"Then you have studied law for nothing. Your taking up a practice seems pointless. Like us, you too could have kept the accounts here without bothering about all such expensive studies."

"Baba, these days the golden chances are available to the Harijans alone. A Harijan law graduate can be appointed as a magistrate much more easily than others. It is also because among them there are still not many highly educated persons."

"You know that a Vaishya boy can never become a Harijan. Well, finish your studies first. After that we will see if ten thousand rupees more can help you secure a job. Our success lies with the goddess of wealth. Her effect is felt even in a forest. It is money that makes the mare go."

The boy left and the Seth entered the kitchen. After he had taken his lunch, Chanda called him to the ante-room.

As he went inside, she closed the door. She spoke in a whisper, "Three thousand rupees in cash and currency notes worth about 10,000."

"Anything else?"

"There are the mortgaged ornaments. He estimated their weight to be about thirty tolas. There must be about six kilos of silver. Better call Lala and ask him to sell all the ornaments. It does not matter if tomorrow a hue and cry is raised for them. No ornaments, no trouble. It's a period of depression and the rate is about twelve thousand. Multiplied by three, that comes to thirty-six thousand rupees. Earlier the rate was fourteen thousand. In the marriage season it will again be as before."

The Seth's eyes shone with greed. He came out and sat on his own cushion. He said to Girdhari, "Go, have your lunch, and also look for any mail on your way back."

Sinath was going toward Dhanji's shop. Half-way there he happened to meet the headmaster of the school. He was from U.P. and in his thirties. They were on very good terms with each other.

"Matsahab, where are you going? Do you stay at Dhanji's place?"

"I was till yesterday, but not now."

"Why so?"

"I have bid goodbye to the Seth. I fear big people."

"Has he grown horns on his head?"

"Yes, and the horns are very sharp. Sinath, you know that I cannot be a party to shady deals. I pay him rent. Even then half- a-dozen boys and girls with running noses surround me to help them with their studies. They do not leave me free even on Sundays. I carried on, even though I was quite disgusted. One day the Seth said to me, 'Matsahab, you must be getting oil and porridge for the school. Why not earn five paise for yourself and through you we may also earn two paise?' 'This is unacceptable,' I said, 'How can one do such a thing, steal from school children.' The Seth shot back, 'No child went hungry without this earlier and will not die of hunger for want of it. You seem to be very simple-minded. You have little experience of life. Your predecessor's daughter's marriage had been fixed. The girl's father knew not what to do. I suggested a way out. I arranged a gold ornament of three tolas, and another one of silver and the marriage was celebrated with great pomp. He has retired but still remembers me. Have you no brother, sister, wife or child? Who does not love money?' I said, 'You are right but it goes against my grain.' He tried to convince me that I needed money no less than others and asked me to be brave and think of it again. I did not want to displease the Seth. It is hard to sit in Rome and strive against the Pope. So I have left the school for good."

Sinath looked at him with reverential eyes. His heart was touched to the core. He mused, "Houses constructed on such rocks alone will last the horrendous floods and storms and even the aeons to come."

He said, "Matsahab, be fearless. It is good that you are out of the mire now!"

He entered the verandah of the shop. On one side in a corner of the white verandah gunny-sacks were stacked, one upon the other.

'This world is comprised of different kinds of people,' says Tulasi. 'Discipline ennobles a country'; 'Grow trees'; 'Limit your family' and slogans like these were written in bold, red letters. About six months ago such writings were unheard of, unthought of. The moment the Seth saw Sinath, he said, "I was about to call you, Sinath and you are here. You will live a long life."

"A long life means greater suffering and distress. I had to come myself in any case; maybe I am here a little before time."

"It is good of you, but how many are sensible enough to come without being called? I fear that a mere talk at times creates complications. One man dies but some other living one is left in a mess. But on such occasions how can I keep my mouth shut? I passed a sleepless night, looking into the promissory notes, letters etc. On the eve of his death the priest wanted me to recover all debts, assuring me that no one would refuse payment. He also asked that funeral rites befitting his standing must be performed. I have no say in the matter."

"All this must certainly be done. The root of meritorious deeds is always green. Even if you have to spend some money from your pocket, you are prosperous enough to do it."

"What has to be done will be done with the support of you all. I have nothing to worry about."

"Tell me what I can do. I want to tell you that I owed Rs. 200 to the priest. But I do not have enough grain and I am therefore not in a position just now to pay the sum with interest at the rate of two rupees per hundred per month. It will take about three months for me to pay it all."

The Seth was upset at this. "The more I praise you the more adamant you seem to have become. I'll see that you are the first to pay. You should know that the money belongs to saints and ascetics to whom we householders will always remain indebted. The money taken and spent is the money to be returned sooner or later. Debts and paths should always be shortened. Why this weakness on your part?"

"Would I refuse if I had the money in hand? But what is unjust and unreasonable becomes harder than stone. May I request you to pay the money on my behalf and rest assured that you will receive it from me in four months."

"Tell me, to how many people should I give money in this way? The priest had lent out about Rs. 6000 to different people. Just imagine that I am out of town or that I passed away a hundred years ago. All the work has to be carried on in my absence as well. My request to you is that your motive now should be the same as it was while you borrowed the money."

"My motive then was pure and so is it now."

"If it be pure, give me the money. Who will ask for it and who will pay it four months hence?"

"I shall hand it over to his successor then."

"If you cannot pay it now, there is little likelihood of your giving it to a stranger in four months. This is unjust. It was written in your hand and now you are trying to evade paying. They will talk ill of you in the village. I shall place your note before the body of arbiters."

Sinath could not restrain himself and he blurted out, "I have humbly told you that I will pay in full with interest in four months. I admit that I owe him the money and I promise to pay it back. I have committed no theft and yet you say that I am to blame. If I am to be slandered, what about your great self? You and your daughter were taking away boxes and bundles from the priest's house the whole night. Damn your holier-than-thou attitude!"

The Seth was smarting from Sinath's words. He was aflame from top to toe. All the same he looked at Sinath for thirty seconds with fixed eyes. He now realised that it was Sinath who had observed them last night. The Seth said, "I asked you to pay, and this was my mistake. You are free not to pay. I did not know that my hands would be burnt even while doing the right thing. I will place your note for the consideration of arbitrators. You may keep it or tear it up. If I bring this up with you again I swear I will disown my caste."

"Yes, do it and if they hang me, let them." So saying, Sinath stood up. The Seth remained seated. He feared that Sinath might prove to be a nuisance in the near future. There must be some remedy for it. It would not matter if he should be required to spend money to put Sinath right. He strained his mind for a solution. The veins at his temples were distended and his head was hot. His mind was working overtime. He knew not how to proceed.

At last he made up his mind. He mused, "It's a thief alone that catches a thief. I'll do nothing myself. Let somebody else strike for me. One blow will make me happy and two happier still." He was now steady enough to go home.

5

In the morning about half-a-dozen girls between the age of ten and twelve gathered in Dhanji's compound. Many of them were wearing dirty shorts. They were bare-headed. Thcir hair was stiff with dirt and knotted. Their faces were patchy because of malnourishment, the scorching sun and cold winds. Layers of filth on their bellies and the bareness of their feet told their story. Two of them had on filthy coats that were all but torn. Soon as many as there were girls there, that many women turned up. All of them had small earthen bowls in their hands and somewhat bigger black-bottomed vessels of aluminium. Most of them had packages of green grass weighing about three kilos each on their heads. Almost all of them were from Nayak and Meghwal families. One of them was a Dholi. They had gathered there for buttermilk.

In front of the northern gate there was a low square seat over which there was a low wooden chair-like structure without a back- rest. The Seth's wife was seated in her chair. She was a woman in her early seventies. She had with her a big iron vessel which could hold about 15 kilograms and a smaller-round, wooden scoop which could hold about half-a-kilo of buttermilk. The buttermilk was watered down to a thin consistency. It was to be used as payment for the green grass that these women brought. It was all very carefully measured out, and no grass meant a flat refusal from the Sethani.

A girl stood near the seat of the mistress of the house. She said, "Grandmother, let me have some."

"Where is your package of grass?"

"I have already dropped it into the cow-shed."

"You are telling a lie. Show it to me."

The girl brought her bundle from the shed for inspection.

"This does not measure up to even two morsels for a cow. Bring at least some mouthfuls."

"From tomorrow I will fetch double this weight."

"Take this and hold your tongue. Don't I know what you are!" She poured out a small measure of buttermilk but it did not satisfy the girl.

She said, "A little more, grandmother. I have brought very fresh and tender grass."

"Don't be impertinent," the Sethani said and poured out just a little more. "Others, too, must have their share."

The other women first showed their bundles of grass to the mistress and then took them to the yard. Only then were they given their shares of buttermilk.

The mistress pointed out a particular woman and asked, "Whose wife is she?" Some one replied that she was Ashu Meghwal's son's wife.

"I have heard that you are very clever at work. Just clean the yard and paste it with yellow sand and cow-dung. It will take two minutes to do."

The woman did as asked. Immediately thereafter came Pandit Ramdhan, wearing his wooden sandals and a saffron-coloured turban. He had five vessels of worship in his hand and in his pocket was an almanac. He was on his way to the shop for religious recitation. He said, "Sethani, take some *charan prasad*. The Seth's wife placed her palm before him. The Pandit recited the following verse: "He who drinks water collected from the worship of Vishnu dies not a premature death. It cures all physical ills. Such a man blessed by God is freed from the travails of rebirth."

Thereafter he poured a few holy drops into her palm.

She said, "Two balls of sweetmeat have been placed before the god's idol. Take them with you." He thanked her for this favour.

"You were to have started the silent Gayatri prayers."

"The auspicious hour is tomorrow. About fifty minutes are especially favourable. I'll begin tomorrow itself."

"After the worship of God's idol at home?"

"My son will do it."

"My son's planetary conjunction is inimical. You had suggested giving some religious alms to propitiate the god Saturn. What things shall I collect for the purpose?"

"I have not forgotten it. Don't worry, I shall be here at 12.30 P.M."

About seven more women were standing, waiting for the buttermilk. On seeing them, the Pandit said, "The Seth's wife is blessed indeed. Where is buttermilk to be had these days? Not to talk of milk, even the water that is used to clean an empty milk-pot is sold. Buttermilk is not there, even to put a mark of it on the forehead. Vyasji had said that there is no greater merit than doing good to others."

The flattered ego of the mistress was discernible in her eyes. What she had heard in her praise cheered her. An oldish woman waiting for the buttermilk said, "Panditji, they are lucky people. Their birth is the result of their accumulated merit. They always had enough, and enough to spare too. How could we follow suit, and where are the means? We can satisfy our hunger with salt, pepper and curry but not without buttermilk. We always bless them. Please tell us what vegetable we can have at present. God willing, in a fortnight, we will be able to collect beans and the like."

The old woman had hardly stopped, when a Dholi woman said, "Mistress of the house, may you prosper by leaps and bounds! May your accounts run to crores of rupees. There is no buttermilk in the village. In most houses there are no more churning pots and most of them have simply stored them away upside down. Below them, squirrels and rats now play hide and seek. Buttermilk is to be had either here or at Hazarimal's place. Their life is blessed for nourishing people like us... Let me also have some buttermilk so that I can wet my bread in it. The *laddoos* are so stale and hard that even a stone cannot break them. How else can I eat them ? They were given to me day before yesterday."

"But you have brought no grass."

"My feet are aching. Even walking here meant a great stain, otherwise I would have gladly brought you fresh green grass. The children will do it tomorrow. They loaf about with the others and do not have the sense to even offer water to old people." She was given three quarters of a bowl.

A girl who was not given buttermilk did not move from where she was. The Sethani said, "Whose daughter is she? How shamelessly she has made the seat her own? You like buttermilk but not the green grass which the animals need. You didn't bring any yesterday either?"

The girl looked at her helpless and silent. When she looked at her empty pot a black shadow crossed her face, a reflection of the fear in her heart. Who was there to sympathise with her? Her mother is dead. The stepmother's heart could never melt for her. She had told the girl, "If you return without buttermilk I will not let you enter the house." She did not care that the Sethani would not let her even look at the buttermilk without paying the 'tax'. At home her stepmother had kept her busy mixing the dung into a mortar. She had been left with no free time in which to fetch the grass. As the Sethani was to rise from her seat the girl said, "Tomorrow, I too will bring you green grass."

"You will bring sand from the dunes," the Sethani said and poured a quarter of a seer of the wash into her bowl.

Hazarimal was no different from Dhanji. His wife had fasted for two, three and even eight days on many occasions. She was willing to observe such rites again. Several times she had fed relatives and friends and would give measures of buttermilk to the poor. In the rainy season farmers had to part with grass, leaves, vegetables like 'sangari', 'kair', 'fog' and other produce, but the return would be just buttermilk. Their poverty rendered them poorer still, making the rich richer without any effort on their part. Even what they would sell, it had to be at cheaper rates because of their dependence on the rich!

Hazarimal's advice was, "It is not wise to purchase green grass. In the jungle so much grass grows that it is for the taking, but such a mean job is not for the rich. In pouring buttermilk if our hands are not worn out, how can theirs be in bringing small packages of grass? What belongs to the cows is given to the poor. What is obtained in return has got to be the animals' rightful share."

Ramdhan who was standing nearby said, "Your logic is simply irrefutable."

"Oh, no. Their needs are fulfilled and our purpose is served."

"Your name will shine. I need not tell you that the root of good deeds is ever green."

"One does earn merit in nourishing the poor and refreshing them with buttermilk."

That motherless girl, who had been the last to get a portion of buttermilk, drank with relish as much buttermilk as she could hold in her palm. It tasted sweet. She was tempted to drink up all that was in the bowl but did not, for fear of her stepmother. She went and stood near where the Sethani was seated. Nobody noticed her for a full fifteen minutes. At last a boy saw her and said, "Grandmother, that girl who always comes here is standing outside."

"Oh Heavens, she will not budge without taking some buttermilk. But who opened the gate to her? Just give her a little and ask her to leave forthwith."

The boy poured out a little white, watery stuff and said to her, "Next time you come like this, I'll thrash you."

Three women who had taken buttermilk were coming out of Dhanji's house when they saw Kanha Kotwal's son's wife. She had applied black powder to colour her teeth and her lips were reddened. Her *chappals* were red. A woman said to her, "Madam, grace us too with a little buttermilk. You have a say in the household."

"What do you think? Am I the mistress of the house?"

"We think of you as no less than the mistress," she said and moved on.

The mistress was sitting in an armless seat drinking tea, when three sweeper-women came before her. One of them said, "You have given me only a rupee for the month. Please give me a full- sleeved blouse."

The mistress turned her seat around, so that her back was turned to the sweeper. Soon after that Dhanji's wife arrived. She was not less than a quintal in weight. She said, "We gave you a blouse ten days back. It had been worn for less than a month. Do we run a cloth-mill here? We give you your daily meal and in addition a rupee per month."

"Then I shall be forced to work elsewhere, because I just cannot manage on what you give me. Henceforth I will take two rupees. One rupee will not do."

"Do you think rupees grow on trees ?"

"You are now fifteen people in the house, may your numbers multiply! When you were only half the number I was given a rupee to pick up the rubbish and clean the toilet and now when you are fifteen, then too I am paid the same. You gave us an old, worn out underwear for our grandson. We took it as if it were gold lace, but only day before yesterday his new shorts were eaten by a calf. Who can we blame for this? In any case, please tell me who else can do our work. Everybody has his own vocation, and we have ours, which no one else is prepared to do."

The sweeper-woman's grandson aged twelve came up to them. He said, "Grandmother, as you told me, I removed two dead pigeons from the verandah yesterday. Please let me have my wages for it."

"Why have you come to torture me thus?" She rose and opened a tiffin carrier, took out two *laddoos* made of sesame and jaggery which had been prepared on the occasion of the transition of the sun from one side of the zodiac which had taken place seven months ago. She gave them to the boy. He bit hard on one but to no effect. He said, "Grandma, what sweetmeat is this?"

"Do you expect me to prepare fresh ones in a big boiling pan? They are as good as any others. Break them with a stone." In the mean time Dhanji approached, and said, "Nathia's mother, what is all this noise about?"

"Master, our stomach is the same as that of others. When it is not filled, we have got to open our mouth a little."

"The village is big enough to fill your stomach. Is it a stomach or a godown?"

"If the village is big, shall I lift it on my head? If we receive loaves from ten houses, we can make do for only one meal, since they are as thin as skin. Our evenings are bleak. You are aware of the spiralling prices. You sell just a little oil for eight annas. It is not enough to season even a single vegetable boiled with spices. And what about tea? Who can do without tea? Nor can we do without chillies and condiments. What we receive, all told, is meagre. Why should you be strict towards us alone? May God bless you with added prosperity!"

The sweeper-woman's son came forward again and said, "The rubbish from your house alone is a full donkey-load. One rupee means nothing. It must be trebled. Jats, landlords and the like are to be preferred as employers. It is on rare occasions that we remove a dead cat or dog. For this small job we are given rewards on occasions like Holi and Diwali. Besides that they give us what is their settled practice in this regard."

The Seth said, "The son is smarter than the mother. Loot us and feel happy."

"No, master. Please do not be so harsh. You are generous donors. May you thrive! We receive but what you give. It is beneath your dignity to account for it in such a manner."

"It's all right. Go on doing your work regularly and on time. We will pay you one more rupee."

The mother and son were off. And now came the Settlement Officer to say, "Your presence is needed. The police Sub-Inspector is here."

The Seth was startled for a minute and then pulling himself together said, "Bhoma, what is special today?"

"I don't quite know, but from the talk going around it must be related to sterilization."

The Seth went with him. The Sarpanch, police-sub-inspector, Patwari, village Sewak, and some influential people of the village, including Hazarimal, were assembled there. He wished them and sat on one side.

The Police Officer said, "Welcome, all of you. Listen, please. The Government is very strict regarding sterilization. No government servant, when sighted, is spared, notwithstanding his being strongly recommended. If somebody were to make the slightest protest he is suspended then and there or his salary is stopped. If he were to make a fuss, he is compulsorily retired. The Tehsildar and Nazim give judgement then and there. The Peshkar and Patwari are of one mind. The Court is quite close to the vasectomy camp. Who dares fight the government? Persuade people to come forward or else force will have to be used."

They were all listening to him intently and stared at him. The Police Officer stared back at them in an awe-inspiring manner and guessed that his word had had the desired effect. He spoke again in his premptory manner, "The officers have told me in unmistakable terms that my circle must bring in 160 cases, using whatever means I choose. If I fail, I will be dubbed inefficient and it may also damage my service record. I request the Patwari and Gram sewak to bring with them two men each by 8 A.M. or latest by noon. Those willing for sterlization will receive sixty rupees each. We will take them in a jeep and the next day take them back to their houses." He then said to the two rich Seths, "You too also arrange two people each." "Don't you do business in mortgaging properties and earning interest?"

"Yes, we do," they agreed.

"Have you your licence for that?"

"No, Sir."

"Then any day you may find yourself in a police lock-up."

Both the Seths looked at him in consternation and fear. They became very nervous. The police officer said, "So help the government with all your might. It should be easy enough to persuade your clients. Tell me if you have some case of your own where you need my help."

"We assure you we will do our best."

"Even if you have to spend some money from your pocket, do not hesitate, otherwise you yourself may be embroiled in a mess."

Hazarimal said, "We...we are past that age."

The police officer interrupted and said, "Age is no consideration. The quota must be completed." He said to the Sarpanch, "You may go now and I shall take about a dozen people with me. Report all protest cases."

They all moved off in quest of victims. The Patwari had his eye on some. The Sarpanch had to settle old scores with some others; now was the golden opportunity, to fix them. Hazarimal said, "Come on, the government is blind and may cause trouble to us even in our old age."

Dhanji said, "Friend, pall-bearers also burn sometimes with the dead body. Whatever be the government, our currency can never be dishonoured. We are sons of the goddess of wealth. A fox can take recourse to a hundred thousand ways." Hazarimal said laughing, "What nuptial celebrations are we to perform for ourselves? We have heard that a mutilated person is rendered unfit for all sacrifices."

A Sadh boy of about twenty-two stayed near Hazarimal's house. He was born blind but was very adept at work. He could earn so much in a day as not to have to worry for the coming four days. Close by was a peepal tree. There he would play 'Charbhar' or, sitting in front of Ramdwara, throw cowries or dice. He was intelligent but also all alone. In his cottage he would bake two thick loaves and was content with himself. He would beg for provisions when he needed. On Amavasya and Purnima days Hazarimal would send him about 350 grams of flour. He knew that a bully lords over weaklings, so why should he not assert himself? He identified the Sadh and a Kotwal of about forty as suitable candidates to be sterilized. He mused, "I shall be somewhat lenient in interest rates and mortgage transactions. In times of difficulty I shall give them other assistance as needed. After such an assurance a poor man will never object to getting himself operated upon."

Dhanji looked distracted. He mused, "There is a Sadh of about sixty. He is quite innocent and simple-minded. He will say 'yes' to whatever you ask him for. He dresses half in saffron and half in white. He is the right person, for in his case no home will be ruined nor any wife displeased. The Seth said to him, "Saint, please come with me this evening in a jeep. The doctor will just check you up. It will take just two minutes. You will be brought back immediately thereafter in the very same jeep."

"God is good. If you say I have got to go, I will," the old man replied.

The second one to be ensnared was a Nayak of about forty-five. The two Seths then heaved a sigh of relief. Those who dig the earth know their job cannot be crushed underfoot. A lamia captures others' sons and does not give away her own; such clever manipulators were the two rich persons of the village.

6

On the western side of the cistern about sixty yards away was the house of Deepa Daroga. It consisted of one unventilated room and was a poor show of a cottage. Some of the pieces of wood pressed into service to hold up the room were falling apart. Much of the wood was infested with termites. A powder fell on the floor from the holes where the termites had dug away at the wood and left yellow marks on the floor of the room. There were four girders, two of which were cracked and the other two were bending dangerously. However, it was all praise to Deepa that the fifty- year old room still holds. The pot of water and the big hollow utensil of mortar were all she ever had in her mind. The room was left to take care of itself. She had grown very weak as had her eyesight.

In one half of the room was stored fodder for her cow which was to be used when she was unable to move out during the rains. The other half contained her tattered garments, a cot and a small tin box. A couple of thick cotton sheets, blankets and woollen clothes hung on a rope. That was the sum total of her property. The cottage contained a fireplace, a grinding mill, an earthen pot and dung-cakes or other fuel. Beneath the projecting shelf was stored flour. In a few earthen pots there were salt, chillies and some other spices.

The inmates of the house were just mother and son, and that was as many as could have been accommodated there. Deepa was in her sixties and her son, Tola, was twenty-six. Two children had been born earlier, but one died of snake-bite and the other of typhoid. Tola was somewhat simple-minded but whatever work was entrusted to him he did wonderfully well. He was big and strong. He fetched jars of water and also did all the farm and threshing floor-work. He sometimes worked as a substitute, when regular labour was away, and at other times got work in his own right. His average daily income came to about eight rupees, but his mother's hand shakes.

That year, when it rained in the month of Sawan, the room leaked at two places. The water trickled into the cottage from the decayed parts. A big bag of grain inside the room had been drenched. When portions of it hardened they had to throw them away. The rags on the strings had all become wet. They had filled the crevices with a kilo of cement purchased from Dhanji, at the rate of a rupee per kilo. For want of money the cottage remained unrepaired.

Many clouds gathered in the sky. The mother said, "Tolu, what shall we do if it rains very hard? We are so poor that we shall be completely ruined. Bring some mortar from near the side of the pond. In the meantime I shall paste the walls with cow-dung. Rain and death are unpredictable." Tolu said, "Mother, I shall arrange a bullock-cart in which many broad-mouthed pots can be put together. To bring only one at a time means more time and labour."

"Yes, I agree with you."

He went out and his mother started grinding furiously. She securely placed a big pot near her. With shaking hands she was taking out a lump of dung when suddenly it fell with a thud. By God's grace she did not fall with it. A neighbour heard the sound and seeing her sitting on the back wall said, "Are you bent upon inviting some mishap in this old age of yours? Sit down, I will grind it for you. Why didn't you call me?"

"May God augment your family! I stay here under your protection."

"The protector is God, but all your difficulties and distress should end in two months with your son's marriage on 'Ekadashi'."

"A hungry man is satisfied only when his belly is full. I will give you sweets on that auspicious day."

"You must have given ornaments for the bride?"

"A silver forehead ornament and a very thin anklet is all that I could manage, and even this much with considerable difficulty."

"Will the bride's father insist on some other expensive ceremonies?"

"They are bound to demand about a thousand rupees. What has to be done will be done even though I'll have to borrow some money and sell some livestock. I am anxious to see it through."

"We have heard that the girl has some handicap."

"There is no such talk in the family circle. She is gold but for a very small mark in her eye. After marriage, if somebody were to go blind, whom shall we blame? She is strong and capable of taking charge of the family. To tell you the truth even if she were lame, I would be happy to see her move around the floor. An empty floor looks very unseemly. We have neither mortar nor dung. I find it trying even to milk a cow. Further, I cannot bake even my own bread. Just see, while turning the bread on the griddle, I burnt my fingers so badly."

"Look at the size of that blister now. You should have dipped it in oil immediately."

"Unfortunately there was no oil. There was, however, some grease in an earthen bowl. That I did apply. Even then, the blister is there. Yesterday we got our hut mended a little, since light came through the roof, but a proper repair was beyond our means. The rain did not leave even the spot where the ashes of a hearth are collected. I could not sleep the whole night, since water came right into the hut. We cannot get our hut repaired and we will suffer in this rainy season. Later it may have to be dismantled, but at present I cannot even raise a wall. To build a new house is absolutely out of question.

The neighbour woman was grinding away. The old woman was standing in the middle of the floor when Hiria Nayak arrived and said, "Grandmother, let me have my wages for repairing the cottage yesterday."

"Son, please wait for a day or two. Have some mercy. Day after tomorrow Tolu will get his wages. I will then send you your money without your asking for it again."

"Not day after tomorrow, I need it this very evening. I had told you before starting the work that the wages would have to be paid the very next day and you agreed ."

"I admit I said that. I will make some other arrangement if you cannot wait. But why this urgency? Is your house being attached?"

"A relation is visiting. In the evening. He has got to be given a drink."

"Why not feed him with ghee and porridge? What good is there in that urine they call alcohol?"

"Whatever you may believe, everything has to be done as the situation demands. What do we earn for otherwise?"

"Yes, man earns to offer drinks. You will certainly brighten your father's name! I'll arrange the money, so please come again in about an hour."

He left and so did the neighbour woman. Beneath her small hut there was a pot wrapped in cloth containing a kilo-and-a-half of ghee. All this had been collected with great labour over a month. She used to apply little ghee to Tolu's bread. Their evening meals, a preparation of pulses and rice, was smeared with a drop of ghee. She herself went without it altogether, even though she knew that a little ghee should always be applied to bread. She only allowed herself to use the scum that was left when the ghee was made.

She removed the cloth covering the pot. The ghee was yellow, almost saffron-coloured. That was due to the green grass her cows were fed with. She mused, "I did not use even a drop of ghee as Hanumanji's offering. There too, I dropped just some scum. What profit was I going to make by saving two drops? A dead body hardly loses weight if the slight growth of hair is removed from its head. Now I'll have to sell it all. I wonder if I shall be given the proper price for it.I have several weaknesses,such as tea and snuff." She got up and saw the pot which contained two small pieces of jaggery. She again mused, "Let me buy some peels of chillies. At least 250 grams, if I cannot afford more . I cannot do without a kilo of sugar. The oil will have to last for a few days;I'll just have to make do with it. I can manage thus for a day or two, but this is no solution. Hiria will be here in less than an hour."

She put on her head a wound-up cloth support and on it the pot of ghee. She closed the door and left the house. She saw Master Ramdhan near the cistern. He said, "What is there on your head?"

"It is ghee, masterjee."

"Are you going to sell it?"

"Yes."

"Show it to me."

She lowered the pot and removed the cover. The master saw it. The purity of ghee cannot be concealed even in the darkness. The very smell guaranteed its purity. Even then, he put his finger into it and tased it. He said, "I want to take it. What do you want for it?"

"I do not know, you should know better, since you often purchase ghee."

"Maji, I'll give you twenty-three rupees for a kilo. Take ten rupees now and wait three days for the rest. I shall pay you the balance on the very day I receive my salary."

"The rate is all right, but I need the money right now."

She proceeded to Dhanji's place, walking slowly. She sat in the verandah. In five minutes the Seth himself came there.

Seeing the old woman, he said, "Maji, what makes you come here?"

"I have brought ghee weighing about a kilo-and-a-half."

"Is it fresh?"

"Quite fresh, and made from the milk of my own cow. It is not older than a month."

"I hope you haven't mixed anything else into it?"

"I am still suffering from what I must have done in my previous life. How many more nights and how many more mornings shall I see? If I sin afresh at this age , you will know that I have become witless."

"You will remain happy indeed if this ghee is pure. Just show it to me."

The old woman removed the cover. The Seth dipped two of his fingers into it and tasted the ghee. A little he applied to the back of his hand, rubbed and smelt it. He said, "The ghee seems to be good enough. Now tell me the rate."

"Not *seems* to be good, Seth Sahib, it *is* good. Better cook some *churma* (a sweetmeat made from bread crumbs mixed with ghee and sugar) and eat it. Let my chest be burnt if I do anything wrong and sinful. As to the rate, you know best."

"The rate is eighteen rupees."

"Let it be a reasonable one. That I have come to you seems to be my only fault. In the market the rate is not less than Rs 23."

"Then, Maji, take it to the city. Why did you take all this trouble of coming over here?"

"Had I wanted to go to the city, I would not have come here killing insects on the way. Only I know how hard it is for me to come even to your shop, though it is so near to my house."

"In the city you have to pay octroi, many other taxes and fare for commuting to and from your residence. There are numerous hurdles. I must earn a rupee or half-a-rupee, otherwise there would be no profit and no loss. It is my livelihood."

"Please reconsider your offer. The rate is so low."

The Seth called out to his assistant, Girdhari.

"Take this pot from Maji. Empty it and return it to her." Girdhari returned in a few minutes and said, "It is one-and-a- half kilos and ten grams."

"It is two years since you have been doing the weighing. Does ten gram of ghee matter at all? Is it as precious as pipalamul (an Auyrvedic medicine)? There must be 20 or 30 grams of buttermilk in it. Business must be transacted on business terms. You must not be so naive."

The old woman said, "Should you find the least buttermilk, treat me as you would treat a thief."

"Maji, whether buttermilk is there or not, bones cannot be separated from flesh. Notwithstanding all care, a little black sand will certainly be there in all cuttings. Ghee is produced from buttermilk when it is churned. An allowance has to be made for such unavoidable things. Had your ghee been less by a few grams, I would not have deducted a single pie from your dues." Girdhari asked at what rate she was to be paid.

"Pay her at the rate of Rs 18.50. I must give her some concession. I wonder if she has to buy a few articles from the shop."

The old woman did need provisions. She purchased goods worth fifteen rupees and took Rs 12.75 in cash, which she tied in a knot in the hem of her mantle and went away. She was moving slowly and calculating the sum which she could otherwise have received. She mused, "Had I sold it at the rate of Rs 23, one kilo would have made a difference of Rs 4.50 and half-a-kilo another Rs 2.25. Thus I have lost Rs 6.75. All this I did not consider then. Also instead of 18, he paid me at the rate of Rs 18.50 and thus put me under obligation.

It would have been better if the Seth had devoured me whole and I would have been rid of this miserable existence. The religious mark on his forehead is just for appearances. Such are the religious souls! Rs 6.75 is almost Rs 7. He dipped two fingers in ghee and licked it all. Was my ghee curry? And I did not allow myself to use even two drops for my puja. With what difficulty I collected all that ghee! I must return to say how unfairly he has treated me."

She turned back towards the shop. She had hardly taken a step in that direction when she thought again. "Who will listen to me now? Some persons might be sitting there. They will back him, not me. They will call me an idiot and insane. It will be awkward. All these years I have never opened my mouth to wrangle with anybody. I would not like to start a row now". She made up her mind to return home.

On her way home, she saw Ramdas. He asked her whether she had sold her ghee.

"Master, I have neither sold nor received anything. At that time my thinking had gone awry. The money I lost is no better than dust."

"At what rate did you sell?"

"Rs 18.50 and there, too, he said he increased the price by fifty paise for my sake."

"In the city the rate is Rs 25, and that ghee can never be like yours."

"Why torture me by telling me all this? I must have owed money to the Seth which he has now realised in full."

She reached home and put things in order. She rested a while and then boiled pulses and rice together. Her hands were aching because of the exhaustion; and specially with the work she had done with the mortar and dung. In her tea there was but little milk. Even then it revived her spirit.

She gave Hiria the money she owed him. She milked the cow. She poured some buttermilk into her pot which would help her eat the preparation of pulses and rice.

It was night. She mused, "It is a dark night and clouds are gathering in the sky." Tolu had not returned. She went outside. He must have finished his work and then gone to return the cart. It was getting quite late.Shall I have my meal? No, no. How can I, without having Tolu by my side?"

She waited for another fifteen minutes and then called her neighbour and said, "Just ask somebody to look for Tolu, since he is never so late." But nobody knew anything about him.

She went and lay down on her bed. Soon enough rain started pouring down. The food she had cooked would be soaked. She put a cover on it . She took her cot inside the hut. The rain became heavier still. Outside, the cow should be untied from her tether, she thought to herself. She could stay inside to protect herself from the rain. There is no escape for the animals from the torrential rain. She could not see properly and might slip in the mud. She got up and let the cow out. She took the calf into the hut and tied it to her cot. "If it urinates and defecates I shall have to clear it all." Her mantle was drenched. She took it off and wrapped a thick cotton-sheet around her body. She lay down but could not get a wink of sleep as she was worried about Tolu. Her own ill-health was another cause of anxiety. And she was very hungry too. "Why has Tolu not turned up? Has he been stung by some snake or scorpion? O God! O Gogapir! Be good to us. If a person is to be sacrificed, let it be me. Let no thorn prick my son. He might have gone to the farm but he should have told me. I am destined to worry. I do not know how many sesame seeds I chewed secretly. There is no end to my troubles and worries."

She turned on her other side. "If only some one gifted with auspicious features were to put her footmarks on the floor! There's nobody to talk to. It's still two months for Tolu to marry. I am on pins and needles waiting for the day to come." It was still raining. It must have been midnight. She heard a loud sound.

"Has the verandah given way? Shall I get up? But what use will it be since it's pitch-dark. I must wait till morning." Neither sleep nor Tolu came. On getting up in the morning, she saw the broken girders and a heap of mortar. The half-broken walls gaped at the sky with their mouths open. The fodder and dry leaves had become watery lumps. The clothes, the cots had all been covered by a layer of mortar. The long supporting timber of a cot was broken and the headrest of another bedstead had snapped. Two boys from the neighbourhood and three women came by.

One of the boys said, "Grandma, the marriage should be fixed as soon as possible. Your health is declining." A woman said, "Yes, you seem to be worn out. You must at least see the marriage of your son."

The old woman replied, "I do not know when your brother's wife will be with us. Only God knows. Truly, I have one foot in the grave. If the marriage is delayed, I may not be here to receive her."

In the village many houses made of mud-bricks had been razed to the ground and others were seriously damaged in last night's storm. Tolu's mother has not eaten anything for many hours now. Sitting on a slab of stone in the verandah, she looked this way and that. She took the drenched rags, wrung them out and hung them out to dry. The utensils inside were buried under a pile of enveloping mortar. She wanted to go to the village, but how could she with doors wide open? Whatever clothes and earthen pots could be traced were taken out. She was about to leave when a boy informed her that Tolu had arrived. His mother asked where he had been.

"The government men came last night and took about ten of us in a jeep for sterilization."

Walking slowly, Tolu stood near his mother in whose lap he threw sixty rupees. Sadly, with downcast eyes, he lay on a cot in the cottage. His mother staggered and fell unconscious.

7

The tidal wave of vasectomy had swept the neighbouring villages as well. The very sound of a jeep used to startle them. But now it had become truly frightening. People were gathering in the village and the only topic of discussion was vasectomy. Like bees from a beehive, some people joined the group and others left. The crowd was on the increase. One of them said, "What sort of government is this in whose eyes a boy of eight and an old man of sixty are considered suitable candidates for vasectomy? Whoever comes their way falls into their clutches. Tolu Daroga has been sterilized, and his mother is in deep distress."

Another person said, "Bholia Baba of Ramdwara has been given the same treatment. The dumb sadh has met the same fate. There is none to question this indiscriminate and arbitrary sterilization."

From a distance came Padma jat, bringing her bullocks and cow to drink water. She was about seventy-five. Physically well-built and endowed with common sense, she was gifted with children and grandchildren as also with cows. She commanded an overwhelming influence in the village. Her way of speaking was straightforward but somewhat acrimonious as she did not mince words, whether others liked it or not. She had physical stamina and possessed a good measure of land. She held sway over people and was not to be trifled with. She approached the crowd and said, "What are you all debating?"

"The burning question is vasectomy. None dare oppose it. As with folded hands they worship the deity, so also they bend their knees before the government staff."

"Why should you be tongue-tied? Are the tongues given by God meant only for flattery? The only thing that you can do is to croak like frogs without end."

"But what can I do alone?"

Padma roared "I ask you all what do you do except passing out dung? Your heads are decked with turbans, your whiskers are twisted, but there is nothing substantial about you.If you had put on feminine attire and cooked food, your support could have been more helpful. But you are not worth even that. When it is time for elections, supplicants treat you with bottles of wine and bundles of currency notes. You do not have the guts to fight for the right cause. You ask me what you can do alone. Should there be courage and conviction, you can do what others cannot even dream of. If you cannot do anything, what right have you to act as arbitrators? Let us women go there to settle things. We are prepared to face your officers. I happened to meet Tolu's mother yesterday. She was most upset. I said to her, 'I hear that your son is going to be married. You must have fixed the girl and made all other arrangements.' She said, 'What arrangements? An ornament for the forhead and a thin pair of anklets. The marriage was fixed, but now let the Sub-Inspector of Police wear them or the mother of the wretched sender. Who else can wear them now?' "

On listening to Padma's exhortation, Surdas came forward. He was wearing his sarong and a similar coloured loose shirt hanging up to his knees. He stayed at Jagannath cottage outside the village. He said to Padma, "There are few blind men without eyes but many with eyes. That I have to beg from villagers is revolting to me. I do not mind if I am hanged, if I could save a few homes from being shattered. What a life it is when one cannot even open one's mouth? If someone dare speak, he is punished. No one can prosper if he has to live in constant fear. The utmost that they can do is to imprison me. I will get food there as I do here."

Another man commented, "You should know what you will be given to eat there. Your food shall be a porridge of kicks and the ghee will be sharp snubs."

"There is no worse abuse than calling a woman a widow. Let them thrash me. Here, too, I am not a king. I prefer a free death to a slavish life."

Another one said, "The Sarpanch should have collected men and then found out cases that were suitable for sterlization".

" A man boasts when he is sitting in his house. But when it is time to bell the cat, he begins to perspire."

Padma said, "Your Sarpanch is not to be trusted even for a night in a stable for donkeys, and we have entrusted the whole village to him. Bring him before me to spit in order to protect him from the evil eye"

A boy commented that he deserved not the protective spitting, but a dirty gob of phlegm.

Another one said, "The Sarpanch, Patwari and Village-Sevak have gone underground. They will stay there for four days and then return here when the vasectomy operations are forgotten."

Sinath joined in and said, "Grandmother, how long will we live like this? We are no robbers. We must find a way out. Some of us should meet our M.L.A. and see if things can be sorted out."

"Find out who is willing, but in any case do take me there with you. Is she the same lady who wears her hair in a bun?" "She is the same."

"It must be more than four years since we met her in the village. After all, how does it matter to her? You know how many times I accompanied her with my companions in all the three neighbourhoods, and that too without sleeping and eating anything. She had then said, "Maji, you have helped me so much. Tell me when you need my help.' We are not asking her to labour in the field. Here is the right work for her. Let us see if she moves her little finger."

"Grandma, a hungry man believes only when his hunger is satisfied. She is not going to yield anything worthwhile."

"Even so, we must go and meet her. If she does nothing, at least we will know her true colours."

They had already been talking for a long time. The moment they decided to call on the M.L.A., the group broke up and they drifted off in the direction of their homes. Some four persons were still standing around, but they weren't the type to go and meet M.L.As and the like. They had heard that, during the Emergency, even the slightest opposition meant six months' imprisonment and lashes without any mercy.

While Dhanji and Hazarimal were walking along, a man asked them to join the party which was going to meet the M.L.A. in connection with the uproar about vasectomy. Their presence, he said, would add to their weight. "No, no. Who can fight the Government? In cities like Delhi and Calcutta where lakhs of people reside, they demand thousands of rupees for just speaking a few words. The government have shot such V.I.Ps dead. Who will take notice of you and us there? The king, the ascetic, fire and water have contrary ways. Doing this, they undo that. To invite trouble from that end goes against our grain. The government is like our parents. If somebody has got to go, talk to the Sarpanch in this regard." Having said this, Dhanji excused himself. The man reported exactly what had transpired between them.

Padma said, "So far as to the king and the ascetic are concerned, if they want to be away, let them be. Such selfish people have never done anything remarkable. But how could the government men identify Tolu and Gangia without the connivance of someone from the village?"

Sinath said, Grandma, Dhanna trapped the ascetic of Ramdwara and Hazarimal enticed the dumb boy. The blind and the ignorant are both alike. Without spending a single pie, they obliged the sub- inspector of police and freed themselves from his threats."

"The saying that a Vaishya cheats a person he knows and that a dog bites a stranger is not wrong."

"What difference is there between them and the government? The government and the rich both hurt us; the former by forcing persons to be hospitalized and the latter at their shops. The injury inflicted by the rich far exceeds that of the government. The rich hit their victims in such a way that they never quite recover."

"Let them not come with us. We just wanted to see how they behave on such occasions. If in doing the right our hands are burnt, let them be."

The next day, early in the morning, Padma and Sinath set out together for their destination, the bungalow of Kusum Kataria. Within ten minutes of their arrival, Surdas also reached there. He had brought an escort to help him along the way. He was ready to suffer for the sake of the village.

Sinath said, "Baba, why have you come?"

"Don't I live in the village?"

"We would have brought you with us but did not, lest it should cause you trouble. Also, escorting you would have slowed us down."

"My troubles started from the day I became blind and there seems to be no end to them. We blind persons go anywhere and everywhere, but it is good that I have saved you from unnecessary botheration."

Sinath was embarassed, but Surdas could not see him blushing. Sinath said, "Well, it is nice of you to be here; for, now our number has increased by one. The more, the merrier."

Sinath asked a peon to tell the Madam that three persons wanted to meet her. They sat on a bench and remained sitting there for half an hour. The long wait made them restless. Sinath got up and went into the verandah. There was a room with a curtain on both sides. There was another room to get into the house. Its door was open. He hesitated to go inside without permission. He cleared his throat diserectly and a dog barked. He feared that it would come out and bite him. Inside a bell rang and a man pulled the curtain apart and said, "Where have you come from and what do you want?"

Padma said, "Just say that Padma Jatni has come to meet her."

The man returned with the instruction that they should wait on the bench outside. In ten minutes he showed them in.

All the three came on to the verandah. Madam was sitting in an armed cane-chair. There were three stools nearby. They wished her and sat down.

Padma said, "First please tell me whether you have recognised me."

"Yes; but why waste time? Tell me the purpose of your visit."

Sinath said, "In the village people apprehend being sterilised. Only day before yesterday some policemen caught hold of about ten people, of whom one was a bachelor going to be married shortly, and the other one had just one son, who is so ill that he is likely to die. The third man was about sixty and the fourth was blind And..."

"Yes, I follow all that you have said but I ask you not to speak a word against vasectomy. Not only officers but even us M.L.As. have been instructed to intensify the movement. It is just possible that some moist wood is burnt side by side with a dry one. All this must not be made an issue. Vasectomy is never fatal. During the Emergency there is so much strictness that on the least suspicion one may be jailed any time with no chance of being released on bail. The C.I.D. people are unusually watchful. The government itself bows to the 'prince'." (She was referring to the late

Sanjay Gandhi, son of late Prime Minister of India, Mrs Indira Gandhi.) Tell me if I can help you in some other matter."

Old Padma said, "Your voice has much more weight than that of thousands like us. We go here and there with tongues stuck to our palates. We know not how to talk and can never impress others. You are our tongue; so please at least communicate our distress in forceful terms."

"How can I forward your petition when I know it will be damaging to me?"

"It is your duty to convey our feelings to the higher authorities. Thousands of people have voted for you. Will they shoot you if you present the right picture of the village?"

"You are holding me up. Please tell me if you want my help in some other matter."

"Then be kind enough to arrange for us about half a seer of arsenic."

"What purpose will arsenic serve?"

"When we take it, we cannot possibly voice our distress. The officials will not have to run for us. If your cannot speak out, please take me to the person concerned so that I can have a close view of him and speak my mind."

"Maji, you are not talking sense. They have no time even for ministers, not to talk of us."

Surdas said, "In the village the Patwari, Sarpanch, Village- Sevak, their officers and soldiers have all gone blind. They have little consideration for our homes and neighbourhood. Whosoever comes under their grip is taken away. Please see to it that we are rid of them."

"Baba, you yourself are blind and so you are the first to be guarded against."

"Yes, blind I am, but I take no more than three loaves a day, and those I earn. But those blind officers ruin our men. They make bachelors and young boys unfit for procreation.

That's the difference between them and me. It will be good of you if you kindly make those persons act like me."

Kusum Kataria was irritated and showed it. "I have understood what your problem is, but I possess no solution for it. You may go, for I have to leave for Jaipur at 3 o'clock with two buses in attendance. Tomorrow, a meeting will be held which will be attended by lakhs of people." You! Your name is Sinath," she said turning back.

"Yes, madam."

"At the last election you were the leader of those who opposed me."

"My protest was on the issue of liquor."

"Did your protest result in complete prohibition in the country?"

"I had said that there could be no relationship between Gandhi and liquor."

"When you had no faith in me then, what need was there to come to me now?"

"But after having won elections, the supporters and opposition all become one. You are their M.L.A. They are all like a 'ladoo', a sweetmeat, all parts of which are necessarily sweet."

"You have become wise after the event. Your eyes were then riveted on the sky."

"Now your eyes are fixed upwards," replied Sinath.

"Yes, yes get out from here. Who invited you to grace us by your august presence?"

Sinath did not want to aggravate the situation. Fortunately, the telephone rang inside the house. She went in and the three of them returned by the path they came. Climbing down the staircase Surdas said, "Granted that Sinath was part of the opposition, but Padma never swerved from her service. She could have at least fulfilled her wishes."

Old Padma commented, "Even if Sinath was with the opposition, he wanted nothing for himself. His petition was to get the grievances of the village redressed."

Sinath overheard the M.L.A. saying, "Yes, I am starting at 3 by car. The buses will leave half an hour earlier. I will reach the bungalow directly. Where is he? If he's there, connect me to him."

Padma, Sinath and Surdas, with his hand placed on Sinath's shoulder, were all hungry, thirsty, and disconcerted by the experience. They were on their way to the bus-stand. Dissatisfied and with dry crusted lips, they waited at the bus-stand. The bus was to take an hour to start.

Padma opened her bag and took out two parcels of food, bound in cloth,which all the three shared so as to drink a little water after that. Facing the bus-stand was a water-hut. An old man addicted to hemp was in charge of the water. He had a specially prepared wad of tobacco pressed under his lower lip. If you paid him, he would politely give you cold water from a clean pitcher. Otherwise you would get dirty, foul-tasting, warm water from a big iron-pot. Surdas joined his palms together so as to hold the water to drink, but the waterman poured the water so hastily that Surdas could actually drink very little of it. It drenched his clothes. Feeling irritated, he said, "*I* cannot see but why should *you* behave like a blind man?"

"Don't jabber. Drink water if you want to, otherwise take yourself elsewhere. Dont try to boss over me."

Sinath said, "He has spoken nothing wrong. Tell us whether you are here to serve water or to get inebriated? You doze off and your saliva drops into the water. At least half that water must consist of your saliva. And even then you behave in such an authoritarian way."

"What have I said that has made you so angry?"

"You have wet all my clothes, water has entered my nostrils, passed through my breathing-pipe and the throat is still dry. You feel all this is nothing. Then better thrash me!"

Padma standing nearby said, "Are you an officer here? You have been prattling a little too much. You deserve to be thrown into a pool twice or thrice, as we do with a sheep. That will rid you of your drugged state. Instead of realising your mistake, you growl."

Another person said, "Maji, let bygones be bygones. The waterman is dull." He cautioned the waterman to be careful in future.

"He is not so naive, otherwise why does he have two pots, one for those who pay him and the other for those who don't? You give him five paise and he is more than willing to offer a potful of cold water. We just saw a rich man's wife, sitting in a lorry. She was given water in a small earthen pot. Such cheats you call 'Maharaja'. Had there been genuine maharajas, the gods would have come down to offer their homage to them."

The effect of this heated exchange was that Padma and Sinath were offered cold water in a pot. On the front wall was written, 'Discipline alone makes a country great' and a little further on was 'Please do not urinate here'. But people had devastated the wall by acting contrary to the notice. And nearby were heaps of excrement. A few feet away from the wall was a public urinal. Its gate had been removed. There was an intolerable stench all around. Sinath mused, "Such writings on walls, latrines and urinals do not make for discipline. They have urinated over each and every letter of these scribblings." There he was reminded of the Jain 'Navakar mantra' hanging at Hazarimal's shop and also of the couplets, the four axioms, in Dhanji's verandah. They had little to do with the Jains' lifestyle. Such messages are nothing but crude propaganda. Do the government and society subsist on them? If a government could stay in power through these inane messages, what government would ever fall? Even then the race is in that very direction. Lost in thought he walked a little forward. He saw a cartman in argument with an elderly customer. The customer's complaint was that he had been given a counterfeit eight-anna piece. "It is identical on both sides and even the letters are erased. Just a short while ago I bought some snacks from you. Please change this coin. The cartman said, "Put it into your ear to prevent dust from entering it."

"O my brother, I have just returned from the water-hut. You may check if I have any other eight-anna piece with me."

The cartman gave him a mild push and freed himself. He further said, "Get going, otherwise you will have to pay for it."

The old man said, "It is a glaring injustice. You see the snacks still in my hand."

"Shall I deal with you straight? You pose to be a man of means." On one side of the cart was written, 'Long live the Youth Congress' and also 'The young leader is a king of our hearts'. There were other such slogans.The shallow consciousness of the cartman was labouring under some misconception. His face was marked with a crude ego.The poor old man did not come too close to him again, although he turned back once or twice to look at him. After a little while, youth casually made a sarcastic remark, "Do not tease them now. Our life hinges on them. Adore them. The cartman has attended a youth conference at Guwahati from where he has just returned."

The cartman heard it. He said in a challenging voice, "Yes, I have come from Guwahati. Do what you can."

At a little distance a policeman was viewing all this for quite some time. He said, "Even Ministers dare not talk to Gahalotji. Why invite trouble by irritating him?"

The cartman's influence became still more pronounced.

Sinath mused, "See, the country's fate is in the ascendant. Where are solid men now? Creeping insects have grown hoods. Tyrannous, unjust and immoral persons have become leaders. When will this country be on the right track? All governments and leaders shall be judged by their actions rather than by their fulsome utterances. What good will it bring to the nation by blackening carts, trains and trucks with slogans? It is, however, right that the painted letters will last as long as the fake leaders. " Lost in such thoughts, he sat beside Padma. The bus would not start before another half an hour. Padma reminisced, "There were days when Kataria left me no time even to eat a little bit. She would call for me hurriedly and I, simple-minded as I was, followed her without question. Wherever she went I arranged milk, tea and fresh bread. Besides these I would give her curd of buffalo, thick with cream. I coaxed her to eat the choicest of dishes, inspite of the difficulty that I experienced, I believed that what she ate must be reaching God. But this girl did not even ask me if I wanted water. She told me bluntly to get away. You, Madam M.L.A., come sometime and I shall take good care of you. May I live to see that day. If I die before you come, remember that friends may meet but mountains never."

Surdas said, "Grandma, in hell-cats' marriages, the invitees' hearts are relished. Don't look for a comb in the abode of a Jain Sadhu!"

Sinath said, "Our countrymen, in striving for the amenities that are their right have become beggars, or rather have been rendered beggarly. Two nights before the elections bottles of liquor were distributed among Nayaks, Meghwals, Darogas and Rajputs. Votes were being unashamedly sold and purchased. I opposed this tooth and nail. In the name of Gandhi these wine-serving leaders will care a tuppence for us. They are rank hypocrites. What they say is never translated into practice. Tell me if I am wrong."

Padma said, "I have realised this rather late in the day. It's no use crying over the spilt milk."

Surdas said, "Kataria has quite forgotten all your love and service to her but not Sinath's nominal opposition and, that too, some five years back. Like Angad's foot, it is implanted in her heart. Had the ringing of the phone not helped us, she would have got her dog to turn us out. It's good that we were rid of her unhurt."

Padma commented, "The M.L.A. perhaps believes that there will be no more elections and so there will be no need for her to knock at our doors."

Surdas said, "The month of Sawan cannot last the whole year. The winter frost and summer storm must follow soon after. In her conceit she does not realise this."

Sinath said, "She has a bungalow here, another at Jaipur and yet another in Delhi. Her family consists of just her daughter and herself. And then she earns rent. She kow-tows to her officers just as those under her kow-tow to her. To keep their seats secure, this is how they behave. Thus does the line of dogs get longer and longer in our country."

"She has indeed done a good turn to me. I, too, had begun to feel inflated, but thanks to her good company, my silly pride is now completely destroyed. It's a good riddance. She has lost sight of this world here and hereafter she falls into the deep pit below."

Surdas said, "She has no care for religion or the other world. She has no concern either with the Prime Minister or her son. Her only care is to serve the throne. Whether the central power is vested with a donkey or a horse she will sing encomiums of the occupant of the throne."

Sinath said, "I came here once when the Prince put his feet on our soil. Just imagine, one hundred and one gates were erected in the city! The Prince was seated in an open car. Men and women were there with garlands, but only because they were given money for doing so. Officers and Ministers were all in dread of the prince. There were so many jeeps, cars, buses and trucks that the village could hardly contain. The buses came here from a distance of no less than 400 to 500 miles. People had a free ride. MLAs and MPs had been instructed to bring the maximum number of people along with them. At many places slogans praising the Prince were written on banners and walls. The village was decorated from the starting point of the cavalcade to their destination. Who is greater—the de jure leader or the de facto one? But who would make a poisonous snake, however small it may be, his enemy? There were countless people on the footpaths. The C.I.D. men had climbed onto the roofs. I'm told that the welcome cost a crore of rupees. Some said that the figure could in no case be less than about eighty lakhs. Chief ministers and other leader-clowns seemed as if they have been born to sing the glories of leaders. The goddess of learning discarded the poets. Their place has been taken by clowns. Lakhs of rupees were spent for nothing. What good did it do to the public? Were the poor given any cultivable land? Grandmother, a young widow can possibly lead a chaste life if left to herself, but there are many to spoil her. It is just possible that the Prince himself is not as vile as is made out to be. Great men's sons, however, are ruined by those dancing attendance on them. In their names and under their protection they serve their own ends. Such dishonest brokers or sycophants freely use sugar-coated poison pills and do not hesitate to get others' throats slit."

They heard the sound of a horn. "The bus is to start within ten minutes. Get up, grandmother; get up, Surdas, let us secure our seats. They went straight to the bus and occupied their seats. Sinath read what was written on a metal plate in the bus. 'Smoking is strictly prohibited here.'

But the inside of the bus was thick with the smoke of countless *bidis* and cigarettes. They could not breathe freely till the bus moved.

8

It turned out that the rainfall that year was quite heavy. The burning and wilting crops revived. The planted seeds yielded sufficient food-grain. However the weak and dilapidated houses came down and were levelled to the ground. In many of the Harijan houses, their flour, salt and chillies were pressed under the fallen stone-slabs and got mixed with sand. All the earthen pots—big and small were broken to pieces. From them flowed the oil, tobacco and jaggery which they had contained. They pulled their tongo, their griddles, their clothes and cots from the rubble as best as they could. Most of the gold ornaments had already been given to Dhanji and Hazarimal as security for loans taken. The remaining would now have to be mortgaged. Most of them had only boiled wheat for their meals, cooked out in the open. Now were they to attend to their fields or to repair their houses? Those who had some means and manpower would find ways of providing food for themselves in a week's time.The poor and single people locked their houses and made way to their cottages where they stayed during the rainy season. Nearby they had make-shift latrines, urinals and also their bed-rooms. The last resort was the clean sand so as to be free from all cares. In severe winter they will burn refuse and sweepings on which they roasted millet-corn and ate parched grain so as to be able to sleep at night. The really hard period will be just a fort-night, after which they will have beans, cucumber and the like. All this will more than satisfy at least children, if not the adults. Husbands and wives would work hard the whole day in their respective. Children were left at home. The fields were far off from their houses and many of them are not strong enough to bring water from a distance. For their water they go to a pool where the water is black and muddied as a result of the children wading in it. They suffer from guinea worm which gives them smarting pain. Their minds are always in the fields, but they are pulled by the hair elsewhere on one pretext or the other. Nobody takes their side in times of difficulty. When there is abundance of grain, grass and leaves from the bushes, Dhanji, Hazarimal and their ilk will go to them and make a show of their willingness to take them under their protection! More than half of them are reduced to penury. So they go to the ovens on the bank of the canal to work as assistants to masons. There they will earn for a couple of months and then they will go back to their hearths and homes with some earnings of their own. The next rainy season the routine begins all over again and with some borrowing they will again be rendered penniless. Such is their life year after year. These drudges have always been galley-slaves. Such has been their fate since ages.

One day Sinath and Dhirji were in the vicinity of the mud houses and happened to meet each other there. Many householders had placed their griddles on pieces of stone in the open to bake their bread. Dhirji said, "Sinath, many houses in the village have been devastated and these houses in particular. It is difficult at many places to cook food even once a day."

"Uncle, the string that is already broken, breaks all the more."

They went on their way, talking to each other. Sinath's father and two Darogas had quarrelled over a deal about a camel. This had led to the use of lathis by both parties. It had taken place in the desert and Sinath's father was all alone. He was weaker than the other two and was getting the worst of it. Luckily, Dhirji was passing by on camel-back on his way home. It was very early in the morning.The two Darogas were thrashing the fallen man.

Dhirji dismounted and ran to the fallen man. He feared that the blows would prove fatal. Dhirji struck one man with his lathi on the back of his head. The man's nose began to bleed. He fell, almost unconscious. The other Daroga struck Dhirji on the head, but his turban warded off the blow. Dhirji swore at the man and hit him a hard blow on the knee. The Daroga fell to the ground. Sinath's father had been hit seriously in the abdomen. The two assailants regained consciousness in about ten minutes. Dhirji said to them, "Have you had your fill or shall I have to serve you a little more? If you hit a single, unaided man in this manner, the news of your cowardice will spread in the village like wild fire. Tell me why you proposed to sell the camel".

Both the Darogas joined their hands and fell at Dhirji's feet saying, "Henceforth if we dare attempt such a thing, treat us worse than you would treat thieves."

Dhirji Thakur, then in his early thirties, was in the prime of youth. His constitution was robust. His whiskers were black. The muscles of his arms were hard. He was attractive; worthy of being painted in a picture. From that very day Sinath and his relations held him in high esteem. Every year in the rainy season, on five or six occasions Sinath would help Dhirji in weeding, digging out the lentils or working in the barn. Dhirji would always ask him not to strain on his behalf, but he did it because of his good nature and respect for the Thakur.

Beside the boundary of the village the old mother of Suratia Nayak was crying in a loud, hoarse voice. Her toothless mouth gaped open and from her weak eyes tears poured on to her wrinkled cheeks and entered her mouth. Dhirji said, "What makes you weep so bitterly?"

Sobbing she said, "Accursed be my fate."

"Why not tell me the reason?"

"If I bare my thighs, I myself will feel ashamed."

"You are so very proud of your bashfulness, but does it mean that you will not come out with facts? You ought to feel more ashamed of your wailing."

"Then I must tell you. Suratia's wife came with two kilos of flour from the windmill. She said to me , 'You lazy woman, you will not take trouble of even urinating on a bruised skin. You never get up even to take your meals.' I placed the bundle of flour in a corner of the damaged verandah and went out to bring a pitcher of water. You know that no food can be cooked without water."

"Yes, yes, proceed."

"I thought of bringing about 300 grams of buttermilk, if I could get some from Hazarimal's house, so that we could easily eat the dry bread. I had asked the children to watch the hut till my return, but they started playing a game, building small houses in the mud. The dogs, in the meantime, tore open the bundle. They gobbled some flour and spread the rest on the ground, mixing it with the earth."

Sinath asked her when she returned. She said it took two hours for her to return, since she was required to clean the yard and sweep the animal-sheds. "This I could not refuse for fear of displeasing the Seth. My daughter-in-law, sitting on a slab, was red-hot with rage. She threatened me but I was unaware of what had happened. She hit me hard below the ankles with a stick. The earthen pot containing the buttermilk fell with a thud. Some stones sucked dry the buttermilk. She asked me to get out of the house then and there. I cried and pleaded with her to which her reply was, "I'll throttle you if you do not cease crying. When I still cursed my fate, she derisively pushed me aside."

She showed them the ankle where a little blood was still visible. Some dark green spots were clotted.Sinath and Dhirji went into the house. The cell and kitchen were wide open. Some half a dozen children were crying.

Dhirji said, "What has happened is over. The past can never be revived. I am sending you from my cell two Kilos of flour, about three Kilos of grain, lentils and millet too. This kind of manhandling is no good. Bring her inside." But the old woman remonstrated saying, "I shall die here rather than enter the house. I shall have food and drink somewhere in my next birth."

Thakur Dhirji said, "Old woman, such hard civil disobedience even Gandhiji did not resort to."

Sinath said, "If heareafter again you are blessed with such a daughter-in law, you are bound to remain hungry. A bird in hand is worth two in the bush. Do get inside."

Dhirji then said to her daughter-in-law," It was but natural for you to get incensed in that situation but even then it was bad to use hands recklessly in the manner you did. Had she died, the chasm would have been too wide to fill. The old woman went inside grumbling.

Sinath said, "We must help these people at least for about a week."

"O brother, not only we, but everybody should help according to his capacity. Those who are able must help to the greatest extent possible, for they are now making quick money. They will augment their income at least one and a half times.Such chances are not frequent. The poor people shall lose what they have. Those who are evil-minded cannot go against their nature with the result that what we think is never going to happen."

"Why not?"

"They are awfully hungry. In the evenings, however, drinks are provided by one or the other. In the drunken state, for an hour or so, they consider themselves superior to emperors. Our people have ruined themselves in their hollow nobility and supremacy but the poorer people have imbibed all vices from us. All thoughtless imitation leads to such impasse."

Sinath looked ahead and said, "Just see here. The cell of kesaria kotwal seems to be razed to the ground."

He must have the wherewithals to build a new one. "Oh, no. It is well-nigh impossible."

Soon after from a distance came Kanho Kotwal. Falling at the feet of Dhirji and Sinath, he implored them to save him.

Dhirji said, "Aren't you already saved? What devil is going to devour you? Along with you whatever your house had seems to have been level with the ground."

At a distance a boy and a girl were standing. They were his grand-children. He said, "Master, the bitch uses lip-stick and stays at the Seth's cell, in his fence. There she cooks food and is given some vegetable, sauce etc. by the master. For three days she has been absent from home. This morning I asked her to return but she reprimanded me angrily." Showing his elbow he said, "Look here. She beat me with a stick. I remembered my forbears with joined palms. The house is in ruins and always remains open. Dogs come and go there. The children have very little to eat. it is better to work in the field rather than suffer such insults. But who will look after my children? This alone forces me to live, otherwise I should prefer death."

The Thakur said, "Whom does she support, you or her husband?"

"He takes me not as his own and he is not going to be serviceable to her either. He keeps company with lewd people. I had four small gold ornaments which I entrusted to her. Bad days are ahead of me." Saying so, he resumed his wailing. Sinath said, "Come with me. I shall give you ten seers of millet and some grain in lentils. Boil them together. It will last you a week".

"Long live Padma. Day before yesterday she treated me and children with rice and pulses boiled together along with 'rabari'."

The Thakur said, "There is so much dispute among these people.Their language is obscene and they are poor. They are given loans, advance money and title deeds. But what is more necessary is their education which would refine their manners.It's only a good government that can impart such instruction, but it is self- serving and callous. It is the Ganges alone issuing from the Mountain-top that can quench the thirst of the earth. But when profligate thieves and rogues occupy the seats of power, the lower class people lose their native sight. Slighted and rendered helpless, they become supplicants to the profligate. They live on their mercy. Those who are honest are punished severely for the slightest of mistakes, whereas sycophants prosper, even though they neglect their duty with impunity.

"Who can help if their only lust is for power and even then people adore them?"

"But such devotion is not going to be beneficent" Dhirji was going to add to his statement but he stopped short partly because Kanha could not appreciate his views and partly because the latter was worrying for his dying children. So interrupting the Thakur he said, "Let me go now for the children must be very hungry."

Sinath said, "yes, let us move. I had quite forgotten about your children". They took different paths. At a distance Harji baman was seen losing his self-control and making a great fuss.

Sinath said, "What is the matter? Who is your butt to-day?"

"I had given an advance of seven rupees each to Panchia Meghwal and Bhuria Nayak to weed the field. They are neglecting work and always postponing it. I have been imploring them to take up the work but they would not. I had to ask them sternly to return the money."

"What did they say then?"

"They are dishonest. They say that they will return the money when it comes to their hand. They may not earn it in six months or ever in their life. They prefer daily wages in cash to deferred payment. How long can I pursue them? The government has excused their loans and gives other assistance too but their appetite is as acute as ever. They borrow money but have no intention of paying their debts. What is borrowed should be returned in good faith. Not to talk of the government, even if Kuber the god of wealth, showers all his riches on them they will still feel ungratified."

Looking at the poor old man Sinath mused "He is really miserable and despondent. There are many who bend before power but do not care as much when the former become powerless. This tendency of theirs is not in-born; they imbibe it from others."

Sinath, said to Harji, "You are downcast because you have been taken for a ride by them. Both of them are drunkards and gamblers."

"I did not know all this would happen. I have lost both my appetite and sleep. My wife and children abuse me, but even a worm will turn."

"When I meet them, I shall try my best to have the money back from them."

"If you bring them round, I shall feel as if I have taken a dip in the Ganges."

"In future I promise never to associate with such people."

Sinath went home. His mother and wife were busy fixing bricks with mortar. Even though his wife was pregnant, she was handing over big earthen pots to her mother-in-law. The children had taken animals to the field. The daughter, a little away from them was sweeping clean green grass. The cell was in a poor condition at many places and two half-built walls were on the point of giving way. His mother was plastering the wall.

Sinath said to his mother, "Mummy, why not give about five seers of grain to Kanha Kotwal?" Her hands were in mortar, but she stopped work to say, "Are you in your senses?"

"Just think a little. You are not unaware of our financial condition. When will you realise your responsibility? Your father and Sugana went to the field early in the morning, Sugana's wife has now gone there to give them breakfast. She had left her bed about three hours before daybreak. She ground about five seers of food-grain, kneaded it and then swept clean the entire house and now the poor girl, half-fed and without having had time to quench her thirst has gone to the field. There is no mother to caress, console or fondle her. The poor girl has to work all day long. Your aunt is lying invalid. I wanted to take a little dry ginger, but where is the time for all this? It is never wise to borrow provisions from a shopkeeper even if one has to go hungry. Our minimum household expenses per month are two hundred rupees. The daughters have come from their-in-laws. May god help us maintain our prestige. But you are a stumbling block. You think that five maunds of grain is Kuber's treasury. You want to part with the little that we have. The next crop is still far off and in no time the rate of food-grain will go up. In the village there is no dearth of such beggars as desire to live by their wits. Ask them to work and you will find them dodging. Give what you have to them, if only the god of rain should be bountiful." Having said so, she continued her work.

Sinath listened to her. Each sentence was being imprinted on his heart to warn him that he was mistaken. He who is indifferent to domestic needs is bound to suffer in the long run. Moreover, the home is not exclusively his. Who does not toil? And each one has his own likings. He said hesitatingly, "Mummy, give him just a seer."

"Once earlier also I gave him more than a seer and twice I fed him. I tell you that Surdas weaves cots and thus earns his keep. And these able-bodied persons eat well, talk in an obscene manner and have money enough to celebrate a second marriage. The second wife, we are told, cannot do without bathing, soaps and hair-oil and his son dances in a drunken state. If they sell green grass worth a couple of rupees, they can easily make their both ends meet. This year the harvest is rich. God helps those who help themselves."

Sinath listened to her without speaking a single word, knowing that she was right in her assessment of people.

Sinath's mother bid him a cold good bye, but she was not happy in her heart of hearts. She said, "Sinath, in this rainy season we cannot have the services of a ten-year old boy, even if we give him free food. These boys, not withstanding strong persuasion are not willing because of the pressing all round demand, whereas these men of yours are not worth hiring even against water. Lazy they are, but people like you have made them lazier still. If on asking, they are given their wherewithals, why should they labour which necessarily involves perspiration. They borrow, they beg. People like you make them insolvent too. Their poverty and idleness remain intact. You might think that there is merit is helping them". He waited for ten minutes when she continued her work. It never occurred to him that he should hand over some pots of mortar to her.

She went on speaking and doing her work at the same time. After taking his meal, Sinath went to the field. But what his mother had said he could not forget. He heard its echo time and again.

"We really do wrong in helping such people. We first make them lazy. To keep their laziness alive, they mortgage their fields, granaries, houses and ornaments. Later we see them being exploited. Since they are not handicapped, there is no reason why they should not be made to work. Mother is so very old and yet she works very hard. Surdas, though blind, is always seen doing something or other. He is no parasite."

Absorbed in such thoughts he passed in front of the gate of the barber Akha. His chain of thought got snapped all of a sudden when he heard somebody saying'Please come inside'. Sinath went in. He saw Akha and his wife quarrelling. Akha said, "First decide our matter in hand. We will not talk before we are pacified. What happened is that my wife mortgaged our daughter's silver ornaments to Makkha, Hazarimal's sister for twenty-five rupees some two and a half months back. The daily interest is a paisa for a rupee. First tell me what interest is payable."

Calculating interest, he said, "EIGHTEEN RUPEES AND TWELVE ANNAS". The barber said, "Makkhu has taken fifty rupees in all inclusive of twenty-five rupees by way of interest. Further she had said that in her case a concession of about a rupee has been given. That I fail to understand."

Sinath thought over it for some time and then said, "Interest has been charged on interest."

"Had we not paid attention to it for another six months our plight would have been hopeless."

"What was there to feel sorry about? Your daughter had already been given foot-ornaments."

"My son's tonsure ceremony was performed. Sweets were prepared as a mark of worship to Mataji. To-day my son-in-law has come to take his wife. It would have been our virtual death had the daughter been sent without ornaments.

My wife is not expected to mortgage others' ornaments. I sold half a gunny-bag of grain in lentils and gave my daugher a precious ornament Then alone I breathed freely. I said to my wife, "There is little to eat at home and the daughter goes to participate in festivals. Had sweets not been served, Mataji would have barred our entrance. But see this Seth who in two and a half months made a profit of twentyfive rupees so easily. He would have devoured us. If my son-in-law had not come, there would have been complete darkness over the family". His wife said, "Only one's health should be sound enough to propitiate Mataji, which has got to be done at all cost."

"Yes, it is compulsory because Mataji had got a warrant issued against you."

"This tall talk from you!"

Sinath feared that the old man might manhandle his wife. So to clinch the issue, he said, "Forget the past and henceforth be careful."

He then went to the field. And on the way mused, "Makkhu is a child-widow. She has spent most of her life with her brother. Her character is flawless. Engaged in her prayers and domestic work she takes no green thing like water-melon, cucumber, 'tinda', mango, grapes and the like. She does not take raw water as householders do. Her control over the palate and other sensual organs is a penance by itself. But if she is strict in her dietary habits, in financial matters her attitude towards people in distress is four times exploitative. It is just possible that her situation in life had not been redeemable. There are other people not unlike Akhu's wife who feast others by mortgaging their daughters' ornaments. It is certain that they are inextricably tied to the blind worship of gods and goddesses. Like Makkhu, they should exercise control over their taste. Even otherwise they must not outreach their means."

Lost in these indecisive, uneasy and conflicting thoughts, Sinath reached his farm.

9

It was about 8 A.M. The wind was blowing mildly and the weather was pleasant. Women with food for their men were going to the fields. In the baskets along with food were the small children and all were in a hurry. Goading their animals, boys were competing with one another. Their lunch tied in a cloth was hanging like a hockey-stick. The owners of camels and carts were moving with pitchers of water and were making a typical sound when they drank it. The yellow lids of gourd on the pitchers were visible from a distance. A few persons who stayed back at home were busy mending household things. The smoke from their hearths was curling away towards the sky. Fifteen persons, however, were sitting at the village assembly office for about an hour. The Patwari, Gram-sewak and Sarpanch were, of course, there. The share-money was going to be distributed. A couple of officers of the co-operative society are expected shortly. They are all smoking bidis,cigarettes and chilam and gossiping at the same time.

The Gramsewak said sarcastically, "Who repays the loan taken from the government? I know of many people who pocketed all money received in the name of a dairy-farm and did not return even the utensils. Some others took money in the name of leather or some other handloom industry, but built houses of their own instead. Some squandered the money in drinking."

Someone commented, "I know of one who indulged in luxurious pursuits."

They were all aware of the person hinted at.

"Even a blind person knows it all. Many persons left their villages. Nobody knows their whereabouts, because they changed even their names. How can the government pursue them? The utmost that can be done is to attach the defaulter's property. But in their huts - you will find only burrows of squirrels and rats. Only about 25% of the loan could be realised with great difficulty. There are frequent transfers of officers. A new officer may create some fuss for some days, and even dig out old files. The moment he tries to take some positive action he is transferred and his successor throws the papers into the wastepaper basket."

Then came Modia Meghwal. The Gramsewak commented, "Look here, this Meghwal has pinched about seventy thousand rupees and has not returned a single pie nor is he likely to do so."

Meghwal said, "Can I ever dream of facing the government. All this is possible because of the kindness of influential persons like you. It lies in your power to implicate or absolve whomsoever you choose."

Another person said,"But for the favour bestowed on him by Katariaji, he could easily be forced to pay it all".

The Patwari said, "Katariaji herself is the director of the bank. Her writ runs to-day, since she is closest to the Chief Minister's counsels. Her slightest hint is enough to instil so much fear that none dare give the name and address of the person who had taken some loan."

Meghwal said, "What you say is right. A creeper can never rise high without a strong support."

The Sarpanch said, "Last year the scheme was to give Harijans title deeds as also four thousand rupees for the construction of a cemented room and kitchen.

The money was to be repaid in twenty years in yearly instalments of two hundred rupees. The loan also was to be given in four instalments of a thousand rupees each. The first instalment was duly paid. Now is the rainy season and all construction work has to be stopped. The foundations had been laid only up to the ankles. This year three more instalments are due and the repayment has to be made in twenty years. With the change of governments during the period the very system is liable to change and some of the borrowers in the meantime will have expired."

One of the crowd pointed out, "Here comes Ramu who pocketed about twenty thousand rupees. It was a case of blatant misappropriation. When the summons is served, the peon is given two rupees to write that the person concerned is not at home. If this strategy does not work, the village assembly stamps to put a seal on the paper. This works all right at least for a few months."

Harkho Jat said, "The one thing that I know is that entries in government records should be completed. It does not matter whether work is done or not. I have also noticed that some innocent people deposit money with the assurance that official receipts would be sent later. But often they have to pay the money twice.

In our Pachhisa village tell me whether the harvest has been good, whether there is enough food-grain for the coming four months and also grass for the cattle." They all said together that they were content with the crop.

"But the Patwari and Surpanch in collusion showed the village in their records as famine-stricken. About six hundred rupees were collected to be handed over to the patwari, but nobody knows what he did with the money. The village was given another grant of about Rs. 15,000/- for tanks; but they are nowhere to be seen. Few pits that were dug have now been covered with sand. Tell me whether you were given daily wages without working at all." They answered in the affirmative.

The Patwari said, "People like Gopal Nai are to be belaboured.You misappropriate all profit and defame the Patwari."

"When did I name you Sir? I have only drawn your attention to a pertinent point. This has happened not only in our village but also in several others. The Government treasury is vast and all have a share in it. But injustice is bound to be laid bare and I have not excluded our village from my purview. Everybody is naked under the skin. They all want facts to come out."

Jaisukh barber was passing by.

The patwari said, "Have you taken any money ?"

"Oh, no. Why should a woman of low caste keep a horse in her house? I have little to do with such bargains."

"Why not take it now? It's the time when your thumb impression alone will do."

"But, how you torment us at the time of recovery. There is total mismanagement in administration.

What seems favourable now, later becomes unbearable when documents are produced against us. You will then leave nothing with us. No one will support us, for who does not know that blood is thicker than water. You are sure to side with the government."

"Well, you may take no money, but if you stay with us for sometime, it will cost you nothing."

"But what shall I gain by sitting beside you? I shall better proceed to the Ramdwara and partake of sweets made of gram-flour. It is good to face a temple, but never an officer."

The Patwari and Gramsewak said, "Yes, we too, have to go there. Offerings will be made to the deity and later distributed among the devotees today."

They were tired of waiting, since it was already past noon. Those waiting for money had eaten nothing till then. The sun was in the ascendant. The heads of those sitting outside were burning. So they all entered the Panchayat Bhawan. There they started smoking bidies which were being offered by each one of them till their stocks exhausted. Now they were gazing at one another. At last two rupees were given to the Patwari for five more bundles. Some smokers said, "There is nothing like the hubble-bubble (chilam). The straw of a bidi can stand no comparison with it in taste."

The sarpanch took courage in both hands and sent for a seasoned and folded betel-leaf. Side by side there was a circular motion of the smoke of bidis. The smell of a hubble-bubble spread like jealousy and became quite animated. 'That art thou" is its resultant effect. Its taste and smoke are unique, but the pieces of cloth tied to its bottom make all the difference."

At last members of the Assembly reached there at 1.30 P.M. By 4 P.M. people took their money and felt relieved.

By the time the patwari, Sarpanch and Gram-sewak reached the Ramdwara most of the people had taken their lunch. Only about seven people were left. Dhanji and Lalchand, the two brothers were sitting on a thin wooden board. Seeing them they said, "Our eyes had begun to smart with pain waiting for you. How could we eat without you. Come and sit down now."

The Sarpanch said, "I am what my action denotes. A sinner that I am, you need not have desisted from sacred victuals. Why did you torture yourself for me?" Dhanji said, "You are the protector of the village and Patwariji of the forest. What standing have I without both of you? But for you two I belong neither here nor there".

Two Brahmans were standing. Dhanji said to them. "Please see to it that these gentlemen are served immediately." They told him that they would make necessary arrangements. At a distance some women were being served by Chandabai. No less than 250 persons must have had their lunch. . . .

After all had feasted, the successor's investiture ceremony was performed. About forty priests had assembled there. The religious seat occupiers were given twenty-one rupees and a sheet each by the Ramdwara. The rest were given eleven rupees each. Dhanji and Chanda made offerings on their own in the form of eleven rupees to the choicest few and five rupees to the rest. Next day they invited all saints and served them a sweetened preparation of rice and milk boiled together along with bread fried in ghee. All were pleased. They said, "Well done and hearty congratulations on your being so generous."

An old Jat said, "What was served guarantees a blessing. What was given will accompany you hereafter. This is an excellent bridge for the life to come."

Seeing everybody praising the Seth an old Brahman, taking advantage of the situation could not help saying, "Leave everybody else for the present and concentrate your attention on Chanda who is commendable on all counts. She was widowed at the age of about twelve and it is now twenty years that she has been staying in the village. she was never passionate or irate. When she grew up, she held her hands high and fixed her heart on God. Her parents be praised! She has added glory to both houses."

After a little while there was the ceremony of accepting offers from the invited guests. Everybody paid according to his capacity. More than a thousand rupees must have been received which was being counted. Dhanji kept all accounts. The persons concerned were talking in a low voice. "Now things have started moving. A householder became a sadhu and the sadhu became the head priest. The head priest, in his turn, has become a father. He has all amenities like electricity, fans, decorated rooms and the like. Additions will be there year after year. This inevitably leads to conflicts and some third party is the gainer. This suits everyone. Whoever has become the head priest has ultimately gained. Another person said, "They all relish seeing and carrying the hearse. Some people seem to have been born for such purposes alone."

Once, on 'Anant Chaturdashi', Dhanji had organised a festival of whole night music especially of devotional songs and also a feast for many brahmans. They often talk of it in the village. There were plates of sweets and tea. Besides there were fifty bundles of bidis and a kilo of tobacco. The village was never tired of praising the Seth. The other Seth Hazarimal did not lag behind. Four days before Dhanji's ceremony his son's wife had completed eight days' fast. All relatives and friends were invited to grace the occasion. They were served two sweets along with thin loaves and vegetables. About half a dozen old and grown up persons thus commented, "Fasting for eight days is no joke. Even sadhus' eyes glittered gleefully. All praise to the Vaishya daughter. They are repaying the fruit of their meritorious deeds. Such daughters are born to the lucky ones. We are no men. The whole day we eat and defecate. We are a burden on the earth. Even an earthen pot of mash is better than us, for it gives back four times the scarcely ground grain that you put into it. You heat it but it does not complain. The more you heat it the stronger it becomes."

Both Seths are being glorified for their alms and donations, but Hero Brahman and Chhogji Sadh who frequent both houses talked to Sinath in a different strain, "They are too selfish to do any altruistic deed. From early morning to midnight they crush us like anything. Our women work at their houses. We, with our *dhotis* raised above, remain standing stirring ladles in fire which is too hot to bear. Even then we will be made to stand in queue along with others where we are treated no better than strangers. Looking at them, our eyes smart. They never pay full wages which makes us feel aggrieved, but there is no way out, because we cannot afford to altogether break our relations with them."

Sinath said, "Grandpa, notwithstanding your knowledge and experience of hardships you do not dare to speak the truth which is worse than falsehood. Mere resolutions are empty dreams. I will give you my mind if you won't take it amiss."

"Why should I resent what you say? Do tell me what you feel."

"It does not behove any one to flatter a man in his presence and abuse him in his absence. They think that you can perform a variety of daily chores. On the one hand they will touch your feet and on the other hand ask you to take a heavy bedding to the bus-stand. You will do their biddings then and there. On return they will give you a four-anna piece or at the most double that amount. They do not treat it as wages but as their bountifulness for which you will never cease blessing them. Such sheep are born to be fleeced. Shame on thee! You have to neglect your own work and are always at a loss. If you have to beg, why not be a supplicant to God Himself? If your lamp lacks the oil of self- respect, it can shed no light."

Hero said, "The fact is that we rely on their help and support. We eat from their leavings and so how could we develop self- respect? But knowing at close quarters what they are, we cannot but speak the truth. For a long time we went astray. No more can we kill our conscience, so as to forestall the impending doom for our posterity."

"It's no use blaming others when you have come to realise your own mistake."

"We blame not them but their policy. If in case we find our own ways unjust, there is no sense in perpetuating them."

"Grandpa, this presages your rise."

At about 5 P.M. the Patwari and Gramsevak reached Dhanji's shop. The Seth who was sitting got up to receive them.

He said, "Please let me know the purpose of your kind visit."

The Patwari said, "There is no kindness in this. We are easily appeased. Today I have eaten my fill and must digest it before evening. Also I have distributed today the share money. I am moving hither and thither to assimilate the ill-gotten money. You are the fittest person to come to."

Dhanji was quick enough to comprehend his intent. He said smilingly, "It is very good of you to tell me how I can serve you."

The Patwari took out twenty rupees from his pocket and said, "Deepa Daroga will come to you for chillies and spices for which here is the money."

"It's all right. Did you happen to come across Padma?"

"No, but why?"

"About a week back she is reported to have said that I am bereft of sense because of having ruined the career of Tolu Daroga. She holds you and Hazarimal responsible for the ruination of the old man and the dumb boy from the Ramdwara."

"Somebody must have told her all this."

"It's an open secret that the villain is Sinath. We are Vaishyas. As such our whiskers may very well be on either side. But even a hell-cat leaves its own house unharmed.Isn't it?"

"What sorcery shall we practise then?"

"This is not for me to tell you. I have only related the bare fact."

"But you must help me a little."

"Even a thief opens his mind at home. We are not made for violence nor are we fit for the police and courts of law. I can assure you that if money is required I shall not withhold my hand?"

"Such help from you is enough to severe his head without the use of a sword. You will see my doing. It will take no time to click."

"Patwariji, a nod for the wise is enough. It's no use making a fuss."

"Yes, I understand. Now tell me what I have to pay." He left the place. Dhanji mused, "He who misses a favourable chance strikes a discordant note. The Vaishya who does not transact business when the opportunity offers itself is a fool. He will now know with whom he has entangled himself. The maximum amount that may be asked of me is Rs. 2000/-. This will not be very much. I must not seem to be involved anywhere. Other heads and others' shoes! In a fire, what does a tailless dog lose? Let the mill grind. None can suspect us."

He heard his name being called. The chain of his thought broke all of a sudden. He saw that near the door sill Kesaria Kotwal was standing. He sat down with folded hands. The Seth looked at him from top to toe. He who sincerely searches for a thing cannot but get it sooner than later. He thought of something which thrilled him. He looked at him once again. The Kotwal had a very small white beard and only a couple of shaky teeth in his upper jaw. The Seth has been in touch with him for twenty years and had occasional dealings with him. But he never before appeared so good on his own as now. Shoot the arrow. It is good if it hits, otherwise it will be taken as a practice in archery,

The Seth mused. He said, "First tell me whether you relished sweets, bread and vegetables." On his saying 'no', the Seth remarked, "There is a crusher in the house and yet the oilman is dry. The entire village had been invited to the feast. How could you be left out?"

"I had gone to the field and have just returned."

"It does not matter. It is morning when the cock crows. If you were not free earlier, it is all right now. So take your food and tell me what you have in mind."

"I want half a kilo of jaggery."

"That I'll give but I hear that your cell has given way."

"Yes, it is now razed to the ground."

"Your staying on a heap of stones is no good. In the night or early morning a snake might bite you in your old age."

"Where can I shift then?"

"You have no children to cry for you nor a wife to forbid your shifting to another place."

"In any case there must be a small piece of land to rest my head upon."

"And what about your food and drink?"

"This is, of course, the first in order of necessities."

"Tea also you must be taking?"

"I cannot do without sipping it once."

"Cooked food twice a day, one tea, clothes when those which you are wearing are torn. All care for you in your need. For all these things if I search for you a befitting wife?"

"Wife I will have on the funeral pyre. I can't even stand up without placing my hands on my ankles."

"Then shall I find you a really good boy for adoption?"

"Yes, this may be nice but how will he be happy with me, since I have but a field which I can call my own. All else you know, has gone to rack and ruin."

"Your blessing will do for the adopted son, since he may have no yearning for money."

"Then please help me."

"Settled, isn't it?"

"Yes, but only when some boy becomes my own." "What day is it to- day? Must be Saturday".

"Yes".

"Then take it as final, for what is begun on Saturday comes to fruition. Bring your cot, clothes, boxes, and anything that you possess. Give them to whomsoever you choose. Feel free. Occupy the inner room in our fence. You know it. Turn out dogs and cats from the house as also from the enclosure. Food and clothes are free. Take that Kania is your adopted son, though all other children too are yours. If you doubt it still, it will be got registered."

He looked at the Seth for a couple of minutes and wondered whether the Seth had lost all his marbles.

He said, "Why are you playing this joke on me to-day?"

"It's no joke. I am sitting on my seat of income and I am quite serious about it. Don't you see that it is the cushion of

Lord Ganesh? It occurred to me that you should know yourself to be my Kotwal. Every month I must be spending thousands of rupees to get my houses repaired. If I spend a hundred rupees to help you, it is but right since you have served us for decades. Am I not competent enough to serve you even for half-a-dozen years? Don't you know that I have no desire of my own and so all this I am doing is to remove whatever apprehension you still entertain. Better occupy the room today. Keep whatever money you have with you."

Kesaro was thoughtful. He mused, "I have been in contact with the Seth for twenty years. Now I am lonely and my eyesight is failing. As such, he might have taken pity on me. It's no strain on him, for even dogs satisfy their hunger at his door. That Kania would be my adopted son seems to be funny indeed but let me see. What I want is daily bread and a few clothes in a year."

A little before sunset he occupied what was his room now. It was about 7 P.M. The tired people were reaching home one by one. The young calves were anxiously awaiting thc return of their mothers. Cows and buffaloes were no less eager to meet their young ones. Their udders were bursting with milk. Mistresses of houses were returning to their respective homes with bundles of grass on their heads and with their baskets containing empty pots and small children. Some old women and young girls were in a hurry to cook dinner for the menfolk. There were many houses of poor and low-class people who brought stale vegetables and sauce from the Seth against their bundles of grass. Only after that, do they cook their food. There were others who had nothing to save, for what they earnt they spent. The smoke from hearths was getting mixed with the prevailing darkness, but there was light in the shops of Dhanji and Hazarimal. Their business was thriving. The lighted aloes were inserted as a mark of worship to the god Ganesh and goddess Laxmi. The whole atmosphere was filled with incence.

In the backyard of the Panchayat there is quite a bit of hustle- bustle. There are about a dozen people who have received share money today. The Patwari, Gramsewak and Secretary are always uninvited guests on such occasions. Their presence is indispensable like jaggery in the the worship of 'Chauth Mata'. A goat has been purchased for forty rupees. Moti Daroga and Bhuria Nayak are expert hands in cooking meat. Only ten minutes back Kalu kalal left fifteen bottles here. One of them is Suratia whose wife had thrashed her mother-in-law and children so hard that it was difficult on their part to prepare dinner. All this she did just to save the flour for lunch the next-day. The son of Kanha kotwal is no better. His father and children are made to knock at many doors. His wife wanders where she wills. Panchia and Pemla belong to the same category. They do not have the wherewithals to keep their body and soul together.

The Patwari and Isarsingh were having their colloquy and drinking. They alone know when they went away from the boisterous scene.

Isarsingh, in his thirties, is a matriculate. He had been a clerk at the Tehsil office. He was once caught red-handed and dismissed for taking bribe. His father's eyesight was very weak which has reduced him to a half-man as it were. His addiction to drink hardened while working in office which still persists. He has too many children and a field close by. Another field is near Sinath's on the boundary line. He is Dhirji's nephew but separated by one generation.

It was about 11.30 p.m. The village was all quiet. But all of a sudden there was a noise. This was Kanha's doing. He was crying for help, since somebody had jumped into his house. Some six houses away, there was another noise at the Naik's house. Kanha's mouth had been stuffed with a piece of cloth and he had been beaten mercilessly.

Because of darkness the assailant could not be recognised. A Daroga's son was apprehended. The Patwari was seen running. Isarsingh was also one of them but he escaped unhurt. They said that in the morning they would report at the police station. The Sarpanch and his associates reached there as if they were sitting somewhere nearby.

He said "Fools, make no noise. Take some money and keep your cool. We will reduce the ruffians to dust so much so that they will never dare enter the village. There are men and men in the village. Even our five fingers are not alike. Such evil persons deface the mother earth. The defect lies with them and their progenitors. How can we give guarantee for people whose hearts can never be probed by us." Lalia Nayak said, "We will listen to nobody. Even if the entire field is to be mortgaged, some of the miscreants must be brought to task." Some other person said, "I, too, possess a field, I will satisfy myself with the thought that because of famine, the usual fifty maunds of good grain is not there."

Some trite person said, "You must be pragmatic. You cannot sit in Rome and strive against the Pope. Your intent should be accomplished without anybody getting hurt."

Lalia said, "We have our wives and daughters to look after. I shall borrow money from Dhanji tomorrow morning and approach the police station whether you like it or not."

The commotion lasted till 2 a.m. Every year such incidents come to light. There is, however, much less noise during the day than at night. The two Seths have nothing to lose but everything to gain. Others' adversity is their prosperity.

10

The field is ripe. The Kharif crops are excellent. Winds injurious to crops have been blowing for three days. It has destroyed grain which otherwise nobody would have bothered about.

Grass, scattered or a little stale, is reaching Dhanji's place for being cut. Fifty carts have dropped two heaps and at least three more will reach there. In the village a cart is estimated to carry about ten maunds of grass but those who bring grass for Dhanji and Hazarimal do not bring less than twelve maunds on an average. In secret there are some favourites of them who bring fifteen maunds per cart. The cart-fare is overtly the same, but these two keep separate accounts to facilitate their indulgence in black-marketing. They give one rupee more than the stipulated rate and about half a Kilogramme of black jaggery for bullocks. The poor people raise a hue and cry but mere noise without money and land does not work.

Nathu Godara had just been to Dhanji. He said, "Your Honour, one hundred and sixty maunds of fine grass and sixteen carts were there in the open. But curiously enough, they were taken as eleven only. Is this the way of living? In case we have this much for ourselves, the count will be more than twenty carts and consequently increased cartage fare."

"Just see, Chaudhari, the rule is that others' plates seem more enticing than your own, even though there may be no difference between the two. It seems to you that we have taken much more grass than the actual weight would warrant whereas it seems to me that I have received somewhat less than the count. The scales are there in the fence which neither you nor I can manipulate. Get it weighed in your presence and take money to the last pie. Why should you propagate such things in the village, and why should you feel small in any way? We take nothing free and make payment in full. Even then you think that you are being cheated. You may please close all accounts with us. What more can I do or say?"

What could be the rejoinder to what the Seth had said? They will all praise him and pray for his long life. If the grass is taken elsewhere for sale, there must be two men to weigh it, one to put grass and the other to put corresponding weights. As such one of them has to be paid no less than eight rupees. Lunch and two teas as also tobacco all the time. The cart-man will bring about eight maunds of grass in twenty carts but the Seth will take it as sixteen carts only. The bullocks will graze from the heaps. They will eat about three maunds. A maund means forty seers but in the Seth's arithmetic it is forty-five seers. A poor man can never have means and resources to do it all. In this stage of helplessness the purchases will hit hard and the seller will suffer the shot.

Nathu said, "I had merely brought a significant thing to your kind notice. I never meant to blame you. The fault lies with the cartmen. Our loss, if it be your gain, is no loss to us. Even at midnight in our need you alone come to our help. Why shall we sell grass elsewhere?"

"Has all the grass been brought here or some has been left behind?"

"This was all. I shall think of bush-leaves and beans later."

"What is there to think? Keep with you all that you need for household purposes. What will you do with the rest? Better put the money in your pot."

"Shall I put houses in the pot? I had hardly done with my father's funeral rites when I have to take urgent notice of the marriage of my daughter. For me unnecessary expenses are unavoidable."

"You did the right thing as the occasion demanded. The sugar pudding was befitting. The father dies but once. He who desires to keep his name unsullied among his relations and friends must always perform his duty. For what else otherwise do we labour and earn? Daughters are not to be derided or resented, because they bring their own luck with them. With good crops this year, spend with an open hand. My house also is open to you for such ceremonial rites."

"You have ever been gracious to me, Sir. My plan is to do things in a decent manner."

As he turned to leave, the Seth said, "Just listen Nathu. Do send me a kilo or two of raw beans of grain in lentils. You must be relishing this vegetable almost daily. Let our wish, too, be fulfilled for some time."

"Why this hitch or shyness for such a small thing? You will have it tomorrow without fail."

He left and so did the Seth.

Two Brahman women had been cutting chips of cucumber for about two hours. The Seth's wife, sitting nearby, was taking out its seeds, which were being dried on a string by a girl.

The mistress said, "Tea time is over, since it is now 10 A.M. There is no question of lunch before noon. Or are you feeling hungry?"

Both of them were in their early fifties. They said, "After taking tea, there is hardly any urge for food."

"You have to come here for two more days to make chips of cucumber and to take out the grain from saplings. Our Jasala's mother-in-law has a great liking for them. So I must send it to her in Calcutta."

"Tomorrow we have to go to the field to collect our grain in lentils."

"But mine is only two days work. If your grain is not taken care of for two days' it's no loss and I will certainly give you a blouse or whatever. And I shall feel obliged to you for thus sparing me time."

"How can we displease you, then?"

A brahman girl came with an earthen pot full of 'Gwar' beans. Dhanji's mother, seeing her from a distance, said, "Your beans seem to be good. Whose daughter are you?"

She, feeling a little shy, said, "Radhakrishnaji's."

"Yes, this is why you are so clever. Cleverness you have inherited from your mother. The bread that she cooked was no different from ours. She cooked for us time and again."

When the girl was to leave, she said, "Dear daughter, take your food with us tomorrow. Bring some small cucumbers if you can manage and come about an hour earlier than usual."

In the month of Kartika, a Brahmani takes food here everyday. First for about an hour she works in the kitchen. Every invitee has to do something or the other. It may be to sweep wheat or rice clean. If some were to know sewing, she would be given the work of her choice. Many times a girl would be there to pick lice from the mistress's hair. Somebody called from the kitchen, "Dadi, serve food to baboji." Both mother-in-law and daughter-in law went inside.

The first Brahmani said to the other, "We are being fooled, for we lose our daily wages of eight rupees each, with no expectation of any substantial reward. They may at most give us cloth for a full-sleeved blouse, one and a half yards of chintz costing not more than four rupees. And then till the blouse is torn to shreds we will continue to be called for odd work."

"This food, sister, will cost us dear, but my daughter is to be married in two months and who knows she may be of help."

"You have no idea of the ways of the world. She is not going to load you with favours on the eve of your daughter's marriage. Gita's mother saw visions like you. She always worked in the kitchen or at the grinding mill with the result that her hands and feet were debilitated. When in distress she was given a mantle, a *dhoti* and a piece of cloth worth not even seventy rupees, which was hardly sufficient to keep her warm."

"What you say is right but who is to bell the cat?"

"They could easily purchase beans worth four rupees. But what we brought is gone waste, so far as we are concerned. Even if we wait the year round, we are not likely to get any returns. Their hearts can never melt here or hereafter. She had sent Sugani to her daughter in Calcutta."

"Yes, I know that."

"She toiled there for more than ten years. Now because of wind her ankles give her pain. So she was sent back. Now she stays with her daughter at Bikaner."

"Sister, she loves nobody. What she loves is work. Whatever verve or strength Sugani had was all sucked. Now what can they do with mere bones! Even the funeral expenses can hardly be borne by them."

The moment Dhanji came out after lunch they stopped talking. Lalchand had just come out of the fence when Dhanji called him inside the room and said, "This year grass should be in abundance. Everywhere fine grass is to be seen. We stand to gain if the stock of bush-leaves and fodder is in plenty. Such crops are a rarity. We learn that Hazarimal is stocking grass against payments, due to him. "Yes, more than a thousand maunds will reach there. Beyond that I don't know."

"Only yesterday I visited the fields towards the west. They are all smiling but Sinath's field, cultivated jointly, is superb. There is sure to be more than two thousand maunds of grain in lentils, also oil-seed and millet, besides one hundred and fifty maunds of 'gawar'. In between other food-grains 'gawar' is blooming. Its beans are comb-like and the grass stands straight. There is no count of water-melons. They are like stones dug out of a mine."

"But what are we to do with him?"

"Nothing. He owed two hundred rupees to the head priest, but some two days back the blind person from the Bari has paid the amount."

"Why did he? When did the two develop such close intimacy?"

"This I do not know. Surdas came to weave a cot in the verandah of our shop. I had called Sinath's father for payment of dues. His mother had followed him. I explained the whole thing to him in writing. Surdas, on knowing of it, came inside and said, "The money payable by Sinath is with me. I shall bring it in the evening, but if you allow me I will bring it now and here."

"As I said yes, he brought it in a few minutes. He took the receipt from me. I could not quite believe it. Nor could Sinath's parents."

"Blind persons are always vicious."

"That he is. When I offered seven rupees to him, he insisted on eight. I told him that he was overcharging a little to which he did not agree and said, "I take merely my wages but you earn lots of money without moving your little finger."

"I asked him to elaborate which he did with lines drawn on his forehead, 'Sir, you do not bring grass. You do not keep guard nor do any weeding, you do not work the machine nor do you carry anything on your head. Even then all profit goes to you without perspiring for it'. I said, "All investment has been made by me".

He retorted saying, 'Money is no substitute for work. Should the labourers sell their produce as they will, your profit will dwindle. Moreover, even the money that you have is because of the perspiration of many others. Yours is only a sleight of hand'.

The Seth concluded that he was not the man of his liking and that he must be a mischief-monger. He said, "All right. I do not want to discuss anything with you. Take your wages and I shall be glad to see your back. In future I will never commit the mistake of calling you."

He replied, "It will do you good if you do not repeat your mistake. You think that you have given me great protection by asking me to weave two cots."

"Ignorance predominates in him."

"Where does he usually stay?"

"He mostly frequents the houses of Padma and Dhanji. He takes about five rupees and food both times as his wages. He does not eat unless pressed persuasively more than once. An expert hand he is! He does not charge anything from persons he likes. He is religious and repeats the name of God habitually. He has a tanpura to the accompaniment of along with which he sings devotional songs. He sleeps in the monastery of the Bari. For the blind a monastery and a palace are alike. Basically he is sophisticated. He is certainly vicious."

"But it seems difficult for Sinath to take proper care of his field. He must be spending a lot of money on medicines. There seems to be no move towards the police station or the court of law."

"Somebody has played mischief. Neither Sugana nor the old man has come this way to ask for money. So I said to Padma, "What has happened must be accepted gracefully but things must be ordered properly. At present your neighbourhood is prosperous enough. You can easily set apart about Rs. 20000/- if you keep your mouth shut, the situation will get out of hand and it will be difficult for us to live quietly. Now a man has been manhandled, next some woman's chastity will be outraged. If audacity succeeds, more effrontery will follow."

In private the old man was taken in confidence. Whatever money is needed may be taken from us but the case must be proceeded with in the court.

"What was his reaction?"

"What could be say? He laid bare his arms and said. "I can't take any step unless approved by Dhanji, come what may."

Lalchand was downcast. He said, "If the work cannot be done in this way, let it be done the other way. If he refuses to consider the pros and cons of the matter and poses a potential threat to us, let us also not leave him unscathed. It is good that Sinath is not here, otherwise he would have been a hurdle in our transactions."

A boy came and said, "Baba, Hamirji has come from Shyamsar with a cart-load of water-melons."

"Tell him I am coming. Let him sit in the verandah. You had been to Bikaner with Kesaria, What happened to him?"

"I forgot to tell you that the adoption has been legalised. Kanhaiyalal Kothari is now. K.L. Kotwal S/o Kesararam Kotwal. The documents are ready. We have only to bring them. Money gets things done faster."

Dhanji felt happy as his son might become a magistrate without any test and interview. He said, "Let the money be spent where needed, but let it not get out otherwise there will be noisy exchanges. The times are such that records speak, for man has lost his credibility. I must go to the shop. You better call Jethu Brahman and ask him to bring our daughter from Nokha." Saying that he would do it, both left the place.

This is Sinath's field. It must be about 100 *bighas* (a bigha is 5/8th of an acre). It is about 3 P.M. It is five days since he arrived at his cottage in the field. Everybody starts work with sunrise and finishes with sunset. The old couple, daughter-in-law, two sons and two daughters were all working with alacrity. Sugana, repeating the name of Rama was enthusing children and they all dug out grain in lentils with double speed. "Buffalo's curd to Rama", Cow's milk to Rama", Goat's buttermilk to Rama' as he spoke these words to his associates, boys and girls continued repeating these sayings and went on working at full speed as if work was being done on war-front. It was some minutes past noon and all of them collected heaps of grain. Taking fistfuls, they made piles of it.

The old man said, "Sugana, let me enjoy my siesta for some time!"

His wife said, "Finish this work first. The night is long enough to rest. Nobody will awaken you then."

Sugana came with about five water-melons, brought from near the sand barrier against the canal. He said, "The field is almost done. First take some water-melons."

The old woman said, "First give it to Baba. He is tired. He would feel better."

"All of you take, Baba and you too, since you are not made of wood. Have patience. Everything will be done on time."

The old woman said, "Sugana, call your mother. She is sweeping the beans clean in the cottage."

Sugana's son went and asked his grandmother to join them in the feast of water-melons, after which she could rest for a while.

"Will the water-melon taste sweeter at that distance? Is there any dearth of them here? Tell them that I will not unnecessarily move and waste time, which is better utilized in cleaning beans. There must be more than two kilos left. The squall has destroyed it this year." She did not budge.

Sugana said, "Mother has become greedy this year. She either does not get up or does not stop working."

The old woman wondered if she was haunted, and she too, fell in line with her.

Sinath's wife said, "At night she will have pain and can manage to sleep only after we give her a good massage. Even when we forbid her to work, she is the first one to get ready in the morning. She does what she wills, regardless of our remonstrance."

Sugana said, "After brother's mishap, she seems to have been behaving in a strange manner."

He got up and went to his mother. Sugana said, "Mother dear, go home and lie down in the cottage for a few minutes."

"Lie down! Don't you see that there is so much work to be done here? Have I to string pearls together at home? Only day before yesterday you had been to Sinath, but you have told me nothing about it."

He said, "There is nothing worth mentioning. Brother had said, 'Tell aunty that I shall be more active, when I get to lie in her lap. Do your work right and the consequent gain will be mine'."

She was overwhelmed with joy and there seemed to be no distance between the two hearts. As she heard of him she forgot herself. "If Sinath's recovery depends on my being with him, I shall not stay here for a minute. Let God bring us nearer soon, I will then be able to bear anything."

All persons, old and young, are busy except Sinath, who was lying in the hospital. One day the sad rays of the tired sun were shining on tree tops. Standing at the boundary Sinath was cutting grass. About six clusters of plants were still uncut. Isarsingh reached there in an intoxicated state, with a *lathi* in his hand. Everything appeared pre-planned. Roopala Meghwal was with him. Isarsingh scolded Sinath saying, "Dare not touch these clusters. I warn you not to proceed further."

Sinath did not apprehend any mishap even in dream. He said mildly, "Isar, has Maniram gone out somewhere today? These I have been cutting for years and it is nothing new. There is no division between us. You may lift as many as you need."

Saying this, Sinath continued his work.

"This is your unabashed aggressiveness," thundered Isar and all of a sudden hit Sinath with the *lathi* on his forehead. The redoubtable Sinath hit Isar with the handle of his axe. Isar stumbled and slumped near Sinath.

Sugana was working in a water-logged field. Startled by the noise, he ran to the spot.

In his hand was a two-pronged wooden implement. Roopala hid himself behind a cluster. Sinath lay on the ground and so did Isar, from whose head flowed a stream of blood.

The wounded Sinath said to Sugana, "Don't hit him, lest it should cost us dearer than gold. Isar is not himself now, and see who was with him. Inform Dhirji of it and take me to the hospital."

Roopala was scared. He could not hide himself from Sugana who soon found him out. Roopla, however, pleaded for mercy saying, "Please do not hit me. I shall tell you everything." He was quite conscious of his predicament. Sugana dragged him by hand, and slapped his face so hard that his head seemed to turn around. He kicked him hard on his back, which stunned Roopala. Slowly he slumped to the ground. Sugana said, "What is to happen will happen but let me see to it that your intoxication is in full bloom". Roopla became unconscious.

"Let him lie as dead. When he regains consciousness, he will get up himself and go. This much of thrashing should be an eye-opener to him. He will take at least two months to recover."

Sugana waited for a few minutes and then asked Roopala the name of his accomplices. Thoroughly exhausted and scared he named the Patwari.

"Where is he?"

"He has gone to the village."

They went to the village in a cart. In the village there was a jeep which took Sinath to the hospital along with Sugana and Dhirji.

Who could take the case to the court? Isar's father was quite emaciated. Sinath could, but Dhirji forbade him. Even then the Patwari assembled a couple of supporters, but where was the money and where were the witnesses? If the impression of a fist can be visible in water, their intent can fructify. It was only a partial fulfilment of the crow's nefarious design.

11

The Meghwals have their own Ramdeoji's temple in whose verandah a cotton carpet is spread during meetings. The carpet was woven by some Harijan boys, who along with their studies learnt the craft from Surdas. Surdas would tell them tricks of the trade. Their daily weaving added to their knowledge and also to the length and breadth of the carpet. It was also a service to the community. Surdas has been visiting the temple for about a month in order to discuss religious matters there.

It was going to be 7 a.m. Surdas was sitting in the verandah alone in a separate corner. Below the seat on one side, some boys were busy doing their work. It was the 'Ekadashi' night and so religious-minded people had assembled there. Their meeting lasted till midnight.

An old woman came with flour, pulses, ghee etc. All this she dropped into a shallow earthen pot. Having taken a round of the temple, she sat there. With folded hands she gazed at the glass- framed picture of Ramdeoji for a while. Overwhelmed by emotion she cried, "O King of Runecha! we have light given by you. You know the inside of all hearts. You give tongue to a dumb person, legs to a lame one and eyes to the blind. When you fulfil others' desires, why leave me out of your ken? Last year I wandered in forests. Scorching winds; dirty water to drink; bread half baked in a fire composed of sweepings and wet wood; malaria; bitter quinine pills, sleeping on the ground by constantly changing sides — such was my lot. In winter the first two months made me feel desolate. It was followed by a black summer with sizzling heat. With great difficulty I scraped along. I did not die because I was destined to live a little longer. My trials and tribulations were endless."

She stopped for a minute. Perhaps her eyes became moist and her throat was choked. She continued, "O rider of the blue horse! the past days have reappeared. If I think of moving, a chill runs down my spine. But I must go, otherwise, they will catch me by my hair. My son fears his own wife and so I am in nobody's count. In two days time the Seth will get the produce separated and appropriate, the cream to himself. You have given good crops this year. So let me eat at ease for a few days. Leave me at least about one sack of foodgrain. Let me spend a few days without worries. Where can I go with my hunger? My eyesight is dim. I cannot move freely. The condition of children is no better, but I can do little. Baba, whatever you decree shall be obeyed. Listen to me this year. If you do not, end my life so that it ends my troubles."

From outside, the footsteps of somebody coming were heard. Bowing her head at the threshold of the temple, she got up.

Some women entered the temple. One of them said, "Suratia's mother, sit for a minute or two. Then we will go with you." Having gone round the temple, they all sat down. Another woman asked her whither she would go.

She said, "Sister, my husband and his daughter-in-law alone know all this for I am never told of such things. I am one of the flock of sheep. I shall go where I am taken. Now if the god listens to me, I shall be happily rid of all such trouble. I am now a stranger to the soil and so are the people to me. Water also does not suit me. If I am left here with two maunds of stalks left after the food grain has been separated, I shall protect it with the help of a barking dog."

"Sister, if our boy does the right thing, it will make all the difference. Otherwise Dhanji and Hazarimal will take away everything, not to talk of foodgrain. They would even reach before an hour to supervise the thrashing of the grain. Theirs is to take. What power of resistance do we have? They can even make a bridegroom wait for a while when he is to reach the unarched gateway at the fixed auspicious hour. They have no compassion at all."

The third one said, "We will not mind if they take our produce for a year or two, but it happens year after year. The exertion is ours, but not the fruit thereof. Thus, dust as we are, we return to dust. The moment we start making piles of the produce crushed by bullocks they are ready with their balances on carts. There is no pleasure in life and who comes to see what fate awaits us on our death?"

The fourth one said, "How troublesome is winter to us! How we sweep and collect grain by grain; how we bleed our hands because of thorns and splinters of bamboos. We have babies in our laps; we have bundles on our heads. Many times we have to eat while walking. It is better not to cultivate the land at all."

The fifth one said, "When the bread is snatched from the mouth it touches us to the quick, but let us see what Ramdeoji dispenses."

Surdas sitting at a distance was listening to all this talk. Getting a little nearer to them, he said, "Mothers and sisters, I have heard of your misery and like you I also have suffered a lot. I am pained to hear your tale of woe, and how great your suffering is, can hardly be imagined. I will say something if you do not take it amiss."

One of them said, "Surdasji, when did you come and sit here? We did not notice you." The second one said, "Whenever he might have come, Baba, let us have your say. We will neither feel angry nor pick up a quarrel with you. Even if we do, we are going to snatch no title deed from you."

"Sisters, what good can your petition to Ramdeoji or your talk amongst yourselves, do to you? This neither lightens nor obliterates your burden. The plough-lines were furrowed by you or Ramdeoji?"

"All this we did, Baba."

"Who uprooted plants and who cleaned food-grains with the help of winnowing baskets?"

"Who else but we?"

"Who is entitled to consume such grain?"

One of them said, "In accordance with rules the right is clearly ours but it is blatantly violated by Dhanji and Hazarimal." Surdas said, "Who has given them this authority? Has Ramdeoji done it? You are guileless. Leave these things for once. This much you admit that the right is yours alone."

"Yes, Baba."

"Will Ramdeoji fight out the battle to preserve your right and to restrain Dhanna and Hazarimal from exploiting you? My simple-minded sisters! Whose hand will Ramdeoji hold and whose suits will he file in the court? You eat and do you think Ramdeoji will put morsels of food into your mouths? He cannot be so innocent. The grain is yours and the appetite is yours. You alone labour day and night. Keep it constantly in mind that the grain is yours. You can sell it by "Chaita-Baisakh" as convenient and profitable to you. Never sell it in a hurry. After all it's no stolen property. Remain firm. Do not budge an inch from the right stand and see how they dare stand in your way. A certain woman said, "Baba, who is to act up to the dictate of an old person? We are made to grind 5 kilogramme of grain for a paisa. It is only a strong man who can assert himself!"

"When you work hard it is for you to exercise your right. Ramdeoji stays inside all of you. If you do not open your mouth to snatch your right, will you not displease Ramdeoji? Tell me whether you want to keep him pleased or not."

"We certainly want to see him kind and happy."

"Then speak out. Don't remain tongue-tied. This alone will lead you to success."

An old woman said, "These days young wives rule the household. Baba, explain these things to them."

But instantly came the retort from a young wife, "What can we do? Here am I. Never did I sleep comfortably or eat fresh food. Some earthen pot or basket is ever on our heads and agricultural tools in our hands. After marriage, this is our set routine."

"Mothers, mothers-in-law and daughers-in-law must act in unison. Don't blame each other. Ramdeoji will be happy to see you united. When all women, be they mothers, daughters, sisters etc. act together, eat tɔgether, their voice should also sound as one."

A woman said, "Baba, we will do what we can on our part, but let the men do their bit. Some ten of them are standing outside the temple and gossiping.And we will eat a little now and go to the field."

"Yes, do go but do not forget what I have said. No rights can be had unless you fight for them. Convince your other sisters of your stand."

One of them said, "please tell us the purpose of your calling us."

"I want to request you to help me, for I am very much in distress." They all together assured him of all help.

"Just see. It is not a grocer's shop nor is it a police-station or a court of law. This is Ramdeoji's temple where you shall not tell a lie." They said that they would speak nothing but the truth.

"Then listen to me. I am a wage-earner. I work daily for my livlihood. I get up hungry in the morning but sleep with my belly full."

"Yes, Baba."

"I have a happy sleep, but there are many others amongst you who are hungry and half-naked. As such, shall I be unhappy or not?"

"Yes, sorry you should be."

"But I am blind and need others' help, but you have two eyes and also strong hands and feet. I know very well that you work three times harder than I do. From mortar-sand to field work, you do everything and even then you do not have enough to eat. Such has been your plight not for a year or two but for ages. The country has become independent but a living ghost seems to haunt you. Your perspiration makes for their income. They are wholly ignorant of field-Work and even then they enjoy themselves at your cost. This alone makes me miserable."

They were all looking at his face and listening to him with rapt attention. One of them said that they were in perfect agreement with him.

"The buffalo is yours; its feed is provided by you; milking it, turning milk into curd and churning it-all this is done by you and yet the butter that you collect goes to others who resent giving you even buttermilk."

"You have never tried to understand it all. I ask you whose is the field? Who does the cultivation and allied work? Who uproots plants and gathers food-grain?"

"We do."

"Who takes the grain?"

"Baba, it is carried by others" Another intervened to say, "What is this others? Why hide facts in a temple? Why not say plainly that Dhanna and Hazarimal are the two carriers or usurpers."

Surdas said, "Yes, you understand things in their depth, but mere understanding cuts no ice. Who cares if the women-folk can hardly conceal their modesty for want of adequate clothes and no houses for human habitation."

"Yes, Baba. but what are we to do to save ourselves from such calamities?"

"First tell me whether you heartily want to be taken out of this quagmire?"

They all said, "This is our heartfelt desire and believe us, it's no lie."

"The first thing to do is to get united; from the cartman to the axe-holder. The labourers have but one class with no division. Long live their hard work!"

"Whereas one is exploited, the other indulges in merry-making. This must not be allowed to go on. The legitimate right of one is the right of all."

"We will try to act up to your advice, Baba."

"Are there many amongst you who cannot do without liquor."

"Yes, they are, Baba."

"If they are. why not promise to Ramdeoji here and now to abjure wine? If not, they must be held guilty by Ramdeoji. Let them renounce it for good."

"Yes, if we were ever to touch it, we shall rot in the washerman's reservoir."

"Do some of you work at the machine?"

"Yes, Baba."

"How much grass do you cut in a day?"

"On an average, a hundred maunds."

"What does the Seth charge from others?"

"It is one rupee per maund."

"What does he pay the four of you?"

"Twenty-eight rupees at the rate of four rupees to each one of us."

"Do not do it thus."

"Then?"

"Enter into a contract with the Seth and 50% of what he receives should be yours. Thus each one of you will earn about fifteen rupees per day instead of four per day. Out of eight annas per maund, say, five annas are for wear and tear of the machine. the balance of about three annas per maund lines the Seth's pocket. He moves neither hands nor feet and yet earns about twenty-five rupees per day. Is it little?"

"It's really too much. This year we will not let him loot us. We were in the dark all these years."

"Your fodder, your bush-leaves, your grass should be sold intelligently. Wait for two months. It's certainly not a wayfarer's goods. Be fearless and speak with one voice. Pay interest for two more months if need be, but let not the Seth purchase it all when he wills. He should be made to purchase when you know it is clearly advantageous to you."

"So this year we will act up to your suggestions."

"Side by side increase production. Cultivate your fields deep. The more you identify yourselves with the soil the more sweetness will it impart. Make the fullest use of the talent bestowed on you by God."

"We will leave no stone unturmed to work devotedly. The net profit then will be ours."

"It's no ordinary gain. In the coming six years you will have your own cows and buffaloes; you will have a decent house to live in and you will have the proper dress to wear. Do not forget that your hard work alone is your milch buffalo. God has given you the gift of labour which can turn soil into gold."

A certain man had fatalistic notions. He said, "Baba, we will do what you say, but God is nearer to the rich and great people. Without doing any work they swim in wealth."

"Tell me whether the sun discriminates between your and their houses."

"No, Baba. The sunlight everywhere is the same."

"So God is the same to all. The difference between the rich and the poor is not God but man-made. It is, therefore, incumbent on men like you to change the prevailing vicious system." "Now we realise our position. Victory to you!"

"So don't be late and reach your fields." They all agreed and said that the arguments advanced by Surdas were irrefutable.

12

As Sinath reached the hospital, half-conscious because of bleeding from the head and with aching limbs, a doctor said to Dhirji, "First tell me whether they have been sterilized."

Dhirji said, "No, doctor."

"First give in writing tnat you voluntarily offer yourself for vasectomy. We will talk of the treatment later."

"If blood oozes from the forehead, let it. If somebody is out of breath, let him die. First your condition must be met. Under pressure you may get anything done. We will even flatter a fool in our hour of need. But don't forget your traditions. We will do as you ask us to?"

"What shall I tell you? You know whither the wind blows."

"Tell me whence exactly such wind is blowing."

"It is from the top."

"Let it blow but its direction shall change and when it does...."

The doctor was a gentle, simple and practical man. He whispered, "Times are bound to change. God willing, the top will not always remain at the top. But I am like a daughter-in-law who must obey her mother-in-law. We do as we receive orders. The least objection on our part means disciplinary action."

"Vasectomy is not bad because too many children are no good. Dhritrastra's hundred sons will either fight or consume food. In a crisis of this nature, how can you justify the use of pressure as a pre-condition? Anyway, heal them and here I sign the form."

A compounder was Dhirji's near relation. He was his own man and a gentleman too. The patients were admitted and both were allotted beds facing each other's.

The doctor said, "It will take about a month but you need not worry on any account. It is good that you have come on time."

Dhirji came to know that Ramsingh was a surgeon there. Dhirji's son is a captain in the army. He was married to Ramsingh's relative. He contacted the surgeon and asked him to take good care of the patients. Entrusting them to him, he left.

Isar had to undergo blood transfusion twice. Sugana stayed there for two days. The compounder said to him, "Since Dhirji has given me money, you may go. Do not worry about it in the least."

When Sugana was about to leave, Sinath said, "Sugana, we two brothers could have worked day and night and enjoyed our labour. But now you are left with one arm only, since the other is bed- ridden."

Sugana was in tears. The two brothers were very much attached to each other. He looked at Sinath who continued, "But we should see God's benediction even in this calamity. To accept suffering in good grace is to lighten one's sorrow and ensure God's blessing. His help is really our own firm faith, which holds good in all situations. Faith, in its own turn, means perseverance and human effort."

Wondering what next to do, Sugana stared at Sinath. He wanted to say something, but could not for want of words. He, however, tried and said,

"Sugana, you know my desire. In case labourers do not turn up, there must be no meddling with plants, because the earth-mother is bountiful. Let us gracefully receive what she has to offer. We are sons, not masters, of the soil. She asks for perspiration and gives us pearls. My aunt and mother both are considerate to me. Even without me, the children will be all right with your abiding faith, which will give you inimitable energy. Take aunt into confidence. Both of us have sucked her breast and thus, affection has made her, mother of both of us. Keep her happy and pleased."

Sugana started crying. Sinath changed his side with Sugana's support. Sinath further said, "You are simple to a fault. Both of us did what we could with aunt's blessing. Let not our aunt be disregarded. I'll be back in a month instead of two. Just come to see me once or twice in between. Look after Isars field well, as his field has suffered a great loss. At present we are both together."

Sugana went back with wet eyes and a pensive mood. He mused, "Sinath was a god of the field. When he worked with a smile on his face, he seemed to be personified labour which was visible in his arms. His affection for me exceeded that of my parents. Without him it is no joy moving about in the field."

It is about a fortnight since the two have been lying with their faces on the same side. Isar has grown very weak but has been declared out of danger. Weak he was, but what was gnawing at his heart was that, of all persons, he had been rash enough to hit Sinath. They were co-sharers of joy and sorrow. In the world there could be no worse sin than what he had committed. Self- remorse was the cause of his inferiority complex. Though he took medicines regularly, they did not help him much, because of his heart-felt remorse. That Sinath was bed-ridden because of him made him sorrier still. Whenever Sinath started talking to him, Isar passively said that all was well, but Sinath could penetrate his heart.

It was about 1.30 A.M. Most of the patients in the room were asleep whereas some were changing sides in their attempt to sleep. Those addicted to drugs were impassive. Sinath sat in the chair placed beside Isar's bed.

He said, "Isar."

"Yes," Isar said slowly.

"Both of us passed the High School Examination in 1961?"

"Yes."

"Do you recall the room in the inn? Near the latrine, a stinged insect made us smart. You then said the sting was good in so far as it made possible for you to study more for about an hour and that you would enjoy your sleep at home?"

"Yes."

"And what did you say?"

Isar, overpowered by emotion, said, "We might have pretended to read but the stench from the latrine would not let our minds retain anything from the books."

"Our beds then, as now, faced each other's. At the upper end of the bedstead I had placed a tin. My mother had given me sweets which contained pieces of coconut and fried gum.

Your mother had given you typical ball-like sweetmeat and 'rabri'. We had put all those in one tin."

"Yes."

"The sweets sent by my mother were almost all relished by you and those sent by your mother became my exclusive share."

"The sweets prepared by your mother were tasteful to me and those prepared by mine you relished. Our mothers had prepared them affectionately. Your mother loved me. Her sweets must have awakened my living consciousness for her and my mother's spontaneous affection for you must be abiding somewhere in you."

Tears trickling down Isar's cheeks became invisible when they fell on his bed. He still felt shy and shrank from looking at Sinath. These talks fanned the fire of his self-remorse.

Sinath said again, "That love blessed us both.You became a clerk in a Tehsil office and got addicted to liquour. That ruined you, and your golden complexion.Being the only son of my mother I was not permitted to move from place to place,with bag and baggage and leave her alone to fend for herself. I warned you time and again to desist from drinks but my advice fell on deaf ears. That was perhaps not the opportune time for a happy change. Don't feel sorry. God is always good. He has once again brought us nearer which is a blessing in disguise. What you determine now will have an indelible impression on you."

Isar was still melancholic; his spirits were low; he spoke little and wept profusely. Sinath said, "I do not reproach you. We are merely recapitulating our past pleasant experiences. You will recall that on the Sharad Purnima night under the milky-white sky we played Kabaddi. That competition was exciting, you on one side and I on the other. The match lasted for an hour and a half. Stars were high up in the sky. We were twenty-two players. The spectators consisted of about twenty men and fifty boys from the village. Dhirji spat to ward off evil eyes from us and said, 'Come home where I shall give you milk'. And milk we drank. It was loaded with cream."

"Yes, how can I forget it?"

"While returning, he patted us on the back."

Sinath further said when Isar was looking at him, "You should know that Dhirji was a hefty youth of his time and a fine Kabaddi-player. He was known in neighbouring villages as a good wrestler and an expert player. The old have always encouraged the young. Dhirji must have been more pleased to offer us the milk than we on drinking it. My innocent father fell at Dhirji's feet next morning. With an emotionally choked voice he said, "I, father, cannot love my son half as much as you do. At that time they had no cow or buffalo."

There was intermittent pain in Isar's eyes. He wondered why Sinath chose to throw stones in the placid water of his life.

Sinath said, "Like our beds in the hospital our fields, too, are quite close to each other's. Just a call and we could meet in a trice. Our huts on a raised ground looked at each other as if they had had some old affection. As a student I saw your mother with you many times and also with my mother several times. Every time she would give me pieces of coconut, sugar-cakes etc. Where was the wall between us?"

"There was none."

"Did you then want to destroy the plant growing on the soil of love? Love does not usurp anything from you. Love nourished you and was itself nourished. The bond of love between us was unbreakable. It was our unstinted love that won respect of the village."

Isar was looking in front of him, completely lost and defeated. He found no black spot in the life of Sinath, that could cause repulsion in him. He wished to lie under the bed for a few minutes. "But I knew that Isar could not hit me. You did hit me but not so hard as you could have. It is because the hand was not yours nor was the mind. There was some sinister shadow in you. This is why my faith in you did not falter. Tell me whether Isar (God) was in you then. If yes, you are excused seven crimes. Had you willed you could have killed me with a single blow. I know that many times you made even camels turn to the opposite side with a single blow of lathi."

Isar was neither here nor there. He closed his speaking eyes and said "Sinath, the Patwari for days together had been entreating me, saying." I am prepared to serve you all my life. If you entertain any doubt, I will put it in black and white on a stamped paper. It does not matter if my house is sold, if my brother dies, but his (Sinath's) ego must be punctured and you alone can do it. I, a slave to drink, could do anything, however heinous, if wine was assured to me. Not my house, not even the next world existed for me then."

"Isar, I understand it all. I know your nature but the Patwari must have received money from some rich person."

"Dhanji himself gave him more than Rs. 600/-." Once the Patwari said to me, 'The Seth desires that this thorn must be taken out, otherwise it will rankle in his mind. The money does not matter, but the deal must be confidential. For about a month I had been deep in his pernicious company and it was simply impossible to get out of his clutches. Daily I was given wine and meat. What else did I want? Twice or thrice goats were slain. O Sinath, my perverted consciousness could not see beyond the bottle. It was worse than a cowrie, since whatever intelligence I had was submerged in liquour."

"Isar, if there be some thorn still in your heart, cast it off. I swear by the Earth Mother that I have no rancour within me. We are for truth and equality."

"I understand everything but know not how to forget the past. As I recollect, my sorrow is doubled. The more I try to banish it from my mind, the deeper it goes inside. Repentance is the only thing left to me. Sinath, I am very much like a rudderless ship."

"Think that you are O.K. and go to bed. In the morning rays of the sun will instil new hope in you. Soon enough we will be back to our mothers to be blessed by them again. But Isar, do give up drinking now and here. The nasty world takes undue advantage of your weakness. You lay yourself open to ridicule and cause loss to the family. What good does it do to you? If you do not give it up, you will not even know when and where you would be insulted."

Isar now became somewhat confident and he felt sleepy. Closing the outer gate he went to bed and so did Sinath.

In about twenty-five days both recovered and showed signs of further improvement. It was about 12.30 P.M. when Dhirji came. Both touched his feet. He sat in a steel chair between them and said, "Isar, about sixty maunds would have accrued to you but it was not to be. Your father is too weak to be of any help. Womenfolk observe purdah. The children are emaciated and diseased. One day I said to your wife. 'Your inaction will keep you hungry. Start working in the field before sunrise and put your sincere efforts there for sometime. Work in such a way that at least half the usual quota is ensured, otherwise how will you manage things later? Work you shirk, but nobody will lend you money. You can neither beg nor rob others. It's no use dying in a rotten cell. So be up and doing, since the earth has never favoured idlers.'

The children started working a little thereafter. Even then there must always be some money in hand. I do not blame you, since you were not free to act on your own. Some crafty men made you a pliable instrument. But see what a blind man can do. Surdas gave Rs. 300 to your father saying that the field needs his active care and added." I shall take it from Isar, when he returns. You do not know that we had been having joint transactions. You probably know Surdas."

Isar was wonderstruck. He said, "I know him a little but never was very intimate with him." "Even then take it that the money would see them through the year."

Sinath was listening to him instantly and looking at his face. Dhirji took out a bond from his pocket, put it before Sinath to see that his debt had been paid and that the receipt bore the signature of Dhanji.

Sinath said, "Uncle, this bond was with Dhanji. How did it reach you?"

"Surdas gave it to me to be delivered to you."

He looked at Dhirji wondering what it all meant. The money was paid by Surdas.

"How did he come to know of my promissory note?"

"Surdas had gone to the Seth to weave some of his cots. There in the presence of your father and mother somebody talked of the loan. Surdas came to know of it. He said. "His money is with me. Give me the bond and take the money with interest and check it." It surprised the Seth.

Sinath's faith in Surdas deepened. He looked into the note again and again and could not doubt its authenticity.

Dhirji said, "Power corrupts. In past years the chair of a Chief Minister became shaky. He said to one of his inner circle, "I know how to keep my chair steady. Let there be a serious tussle between Jats and Rajputs. It will so secure my chair that no earthquake can shake." And this he did to perfection. The Jat- Rajput dissensions became widespread. It was not confined to the legislative assembly. It had been endemic since my student days when studies were woefully neglected. Many lost their lives. The fire is not yet extinguished. There are some who feel happy only when there is a conflagration. Fight they must; amongst themselves or with others — the rift is always kept alive between Harijans and Muslims, Jats and Rajputs. If a wrong takes place, it is not easily obliterated. If imposed from above, it accentuates. The fight among cats has always profited a monkey, but what has an ordinary man to do in such an imbroglio? He wants a quiet, happy life. Between you two, however, no chair was there to be usurped. I fail to understand what made you break each other's head."

Dhirji could notice repentance writ large on Isar's face. This he took as spontaneous, not an imposed one. Such repentance changes the course of one's life. Dhirji, in his characteristic hilarity, said, "Aren't your beds adjacent to each other's? Both replied in the affirmative. "And what about all other beds in the room?"

Sinath said, "They too are close to one another."

"In this manner a room with another room and all rooms in the hospital are properly, linked to one another.

So also one country is related to another country and all countries of the world are properly filled in the scheme of the universe. As human beings, think of the unity of the world. This will sweeten your life. Be large-hearted and broadminded. Thus behaving, you will not stumble in life."

Both looked at him as if they were drinking Dhirji's exhortation with their eyes.

Dhirji said, "Take medicines as prescribed. All are well at home. Return to the village only when you are perfectly recovered." Saying so, he went away.

One day Pandit Ramdhan came with something deep in mind. When he saw both of them sleeping, he was surprised and also felt unhappy. He occupied a stool placed between them. Both touched his feet and he blessed them. He asked them about their welfare and said, "God is kind that the squabble did not have a fatal end." Sinath got up to fetch water. Ramdhan took Isar aside to a bench in the gallery. There they sat. Isar said, "Guruji, what are your orders to me?"

"This is no occasion for orders. But why this passivity on your part? You did not file even an F.I.R. What accounts for your forced peace? Here you are apparently on friendly terms but I know how sore you must be feeling. On seeing Sinath how could I feel happy? But can contraries ever meet? There is a caste conflict between Jats and Rajputs. Cha, Chha, Ja' Jats are lions and 'ya, ra, la' Rajputs are the deer. If these two animals can ever reconcile, then only Jats and Rajputs can live in harmony."

Sinathia was nurtured by your family and he had the dare-devilry to hit you with a lathi. The children were lucky, otherwise where would they have looked for support?"

Isar could grasp whose spokesman he could be. Even then he said, "You can very well talk of enmity between the lion and the deer, the dog and the cat, but this rule does not apply to mankind. Between Isar and Sinath, between 'I' and 'S' there seems to be no opposition nor is the question of one being stronger than the other. One is a vowel and the other a consonant. Both are like a word and its meaning.

Without their union one cannot speak sensibly. Hence there is no conflict between names and castes.

"Let names and castes go out of court, but can you negate our history? When did Rajputs and Jats have fraternal feelings? Dive deep into history and the cause you will find recorded there."

Isar was going to say that all historical discussions signify ignorance of the milieu in which the events are supposed to have taken place,but did not speak out. But is it necessary for history to repeat itself and past mistakes ad nauseam? Is it a fault to learn from one's experience? He then mused, "By lengthening the discussion what I desire will be kept in abeyance. It's no use putting the cart before the horse. Let me try to extract facts from him." He said, "What shall I do then? You are aware of my financial condition. I do not have money even for medicines. It's the uncle who defrays all expenses."

"No want of money must worry you. A thousand rupees or so Dhanji will give, but all manual work you have to do. If rogues were to have the upper hand, the whole village including us will migrate to some other place."

Isar looked at Ramdhan with a fixed gaze. He said, "What you say is right, but how can I go against the wishes of my uncle?"

"Who has suffered- you or your uncle?" To Isar his real intent was manifest. He said, "The entire village has implicit faith in you because you are a Brahman. But that respect you do not seem to deserve in the least. Tell me whether you have come to lessen or aggravate my troubles?"

Ramdhan sulked but said, "I am here to console you and share your sorrows."

"But it seems to me that Ramdhan is dead. The body is certainly of Ramdhan but the words emanate from Dhanji. I do not worship the body of a Brahman. What I adore is his exalted and resplendent consciousness which you sadly lack.You have come to instigate the nephew against his uncle. Had you really cared for me you would have helped my father maintain the field in my absence and console him. You should have prevented them from approaching the police or the court. You worship not the god in the temple but Dhanji. The Brahman will command much less respect because of your extant role. Please go and wash your sins if you can."

Ramdhan did talk to Isar but he now felt dejected. His legs were faltering and his mind was deeply stirred.His urge for a happy change had died long back.

So some other day the Patwari showed his face. Dhanji came across him in front of the hospital. He said, "Patwariji, what brings you here? Have you come to add insult to injury so far as Isar is concerned?"

He felt abashed but said, "No, Sir." "Is it because of this that you did not file the F.I.R. again at the Police station?"

"I am here for my own purpose." Saying so, he went off never to return.

Dhanji mused, "If I have not succeeded with Isar, let me try Sinath. Nathu Godara is our man. I'll ask him to contact Sinath. He is his distant uncle separated by a generation or two. He talked to Sinath in confidence saying, "It is not Isar alone who has hit you. The attack should be taken as from all jats of the village. I wonder why you took this assault so lightly. If it be financial constraint, I can arrange that each house contributes a hundred rupees, but this mischief-monger must be taught a bitter lesson."

No heart is hidden from a lamia. Sinath said to himself that if he had really been interested in his welfare, he would have come much earlier. He is Dhanji's man. For a piece of jaggery he can swear by the water of the Ganges. Even then to enjoy the fun he said, "uncle, if you hit him it may boomerang on you. But leave these things. Tell me how much you can give me in cash."

"About a hundred rupees I can but not now, a little later."

"Why only a century? Being my uncle you should give me not less than Rs. 500/- if not more."

"Whence to bring the money if I do not have it?"

"Borrow money, pay interest, sell your fields and grain. To hurt somebody else seriously, we have first to ruin ourselves."

He looked at Sinath for sometime and then said, "After being hard hit will you take it lying?"

"If I wail and lament, shall I become a great man? Here is the assailant, Isar.Uncle, our happiness does not seem to be your concern. Your heart's desire is to see me worsted. You seem to resent my well-being."

Leave it if it interests you not."

"Please tell me truthfully whether you have come of your own or on errand by somebody else?"

"I have come of my own, but if you do not believe me, let it be so."

Sinath said, "Uncle, the feet are yours, but the movement seems to be Dhanji's. You need be in no hurry, since there is no question of my hanging you. Now please tell me with God above and also in your heart."

He said, "Sinath, I told that evil man twice or thrice not to commission me to you, since you are too clever for me .When he repeatedly asked me, I had to come, lest I incur his wrath for nothing."

Sinath smiled and regretted Dhanji's intelligence. He said, "Uncle, you have done the right thing. After all, we have met at Dhanji's cost. Please return cheerfully and tell the Seth that the opportune moment is past. Should he insist on stoking fire and blackening the brass-kettle, warn him that it will be very difficult to cleanse it."

13

In ten days they were to be discharged from the hospital. They became very eager to reach their village.

Isar said, "Brother, we are sick of the hospital life. How I long for the village and home! May God never bring us here again!"

Sinath said, "When did we desire to come over here? It is because of the kindness of Dhanji."

Isar was to say something when Padma entered the room. They both got up and knelt at her feet, but turning her face, she said, "You deserve to be caught by hair and dashed against each other's head so as to force you to be hospitalised for two more months."

Both were silent. She sat in a chair and said, "I intended not to ask of your welfare at all."

Isar said, "Grandma, why this displeasure?"

"It is but right. Did you fight at the boundary, win some battle and get wounded there ? You were so foolhardy that you wounded each other. I cannot afford to bear the wear and tear of my shoes for the likes of you. You fought like animals and why should I attend you?"

Both looked at her as some insane person looks at raw vegetables, with a glint of mischief. She continued, "I had high hopes of you when I saw both of you studying. You looked promising. But the more someone is praised, the more insolent he becomes. To celebrate your birth, bronze-plates were rung so much that bronze became dear. Women desirous of singing on such occasions made their throats hoarse. You have proved a burden to your mothers. No less than a hundred rupees must have been wasted in giving to those who congratulated the parents on your births."

Having said so, she stopped for a while to say, "Isar, many times I fondled you, because I treated you as my own son. Not only you but most of the villagers also are being befooled. The Patwari was belaboured yesterday at Kanha Kotwal's house. He will have to lie bed-riddon for at least two days and later disabled in one way or the other. My dear son, this addiction did not remain confined to his own house. He who digs pits for others cannot expect a red carpet welcome for himself."

Isar was much more pleased to hear it than Sinath. Isar said, "Grandma, I adore your feet. How very happy news you have given me. Kudos to you. The news of his death would have exhilarated me. He is a blot on the earth. That insect deserves to be crushed."

"Life and death are in God's hands, but such a man should suffer rather than die. While living, there may still be some chance to improve. Hate the sin, not the sinner."

Sinath said, "Grandma, now is the time for elections.In whose favour does the wind seem to blow?"

"For the present government, it seems to be a wasteland. Even though the Congress has lossened strings of purses at various places, now that people's consciousness has been awakened, its return to power seems unlikely. The stout thick rope must fall into the well, so it seems to me, but who knows God's ways! Our village yearns for a change. Dhanji and Hazarimal are, however, currying favour with Mrs. Kataria."

Saying so she sat comfortably in the chair. She smiled and her face glittered with self-confidence and her innate self-respect.

She said, "Kataria came day before yesterday."

Isar said, "Ma, you mispronounce her surname. It is not Kataria, but Kaṭaria."

"Whatever you call her, her favourable period seems to have come to an end. She hoodwinked many people for long. In the noon, some children said to me, "The jeep is here and you are wanted". I am not a fool not to guess their purpose. I said to a boy, 'Tell them I am coming' and I began to clean the buffalo-shed. I considered what cream I was going to be given there. My jeep is my buffalo. Daily she gives me a kilo of fresh pure ghee. I knew that Kaṭaria herself would call on me in her hour of need, and she showed her face in five minutes."

She said, "Is the grandmother angry with her grand-daughter, since no notice is being taken of her?" "I said, till yesterday you had no ears for me and so today I may have none for you. She is a practised hand in thuggery. She said, "Leave aside the ears, but your eyes must be kindly disposed to me!" I said, "Darling, the day you turned me out, my eyes were blinded. There is only water in them now."

Somewhat saddened she said, "Who can argue with you? Here are biscuits for children and for you a packet of tea from Gauhati." I said, "What is this? What were my children eating all these days? If what you are offering is given to them, they will not even smell bread and 'Rabari'! Please don't improve their tastes! We have to live within our means. What has a dog to do with a coconut? And tea is anathema to me. "Earlier I addressed her as 'Thou' because of my love for her but that day I treated her with great respect. She grasped the situation and felt depressed because of the cold reception accorded to her."

She said, "Grandma, what accounts for your displeasure this time? I depend exclusively on you for votes." I said, 'Madam, be assured of all my attention. As far as I can, I'll see to it that you and your party draw a blank here."

She was startled to notice the tone of the words. I said, 'You have forgotten the past altogether. That day we were beneath your notice. We were not offered even water.

Today it is tea and biscuits but we are what we were. We are no kings and queens now. You were under a false impression _ if winter comes, spring will not be far behind.' She gazed at me. Some six more women assembled there.

Some six more women assembled there. There were four men too. Girdhari, Godara's wife, everybody knows, has been vociferous. She said, "Katariyaji, you move with a retinue of about four people but did not spare my own 'man'. He was sterilised. Now have you come to ask us not to weep and remain tongue-tied?" Other women were on the point of laughing, but Katariaji was disheartened. I said, 'Don't take the trouble of asking us for votes again. Some spineless persons will still cast votes in your favour and that too, without being asked. Why waste your petrol in sand dunes? Kindly leave us free to do our work'. She went indignantly and perhaps to Dhanji, who must have received her warmly.

This time Sinath was pleased much more than Isar. Padma said, "Here I go, you join me soon. We must awaken people not only of our village but also of the neighbouring hamlets as far as possible." She went but not without leaving a live impression on them.

They came out of the hospital at about four in the afternoon. They had been discharged an hour earlier, but they took about an hour to meet new friends. Sugana was there with a cart.

They reached the doctor's quarters. They had contacted the compounder earlier. The doctor was sitting in his room. He was pleased to see them both. He said, "Are you going to leave just now?"

Sinath said, "But for your kindness, we would have departed for good long before." "No, no don't talk this way. I could only give you medicines and that, too, when they were in stock. It's God alone who gives life to the rich and the poor alike."

"Here it is possible just with the recommendation of some V.I.P. or with the power of money. We had neither, it was your spirit of kind service that sustained us."

"O simple-minded men, if one is not to live, no recommendation and no money can work. Should they always work effectively, those with status and money would not die. Day before yesterday there was a case. His mother was an M.L.A., and the recommendation was of the Chief Minister himself. The party was fabulously rich. A team of eight doctors was in constant attendance till midnight. They were hoping against hope but to no avail. Those whom we think as good as dead live healthy for years and those of whom we are very hopeful do not survive even a minor operation. A man falling from an aeroplane may survive whereas another person may slip from a staircase and die. There are, however, money-minded doctors who will go on administering medicines. They are materialists, absolutely oblivious of the dictates of conscience. This leads to acrimony and ill-will. A diseased doctor who cannot do good to himself can never cure others. He will always lack in decency."

Both looked at the doctor's face. It seemed to them that God resides in his soul and on his tongue the goddess of learning is seated. Isar got up and placed fifty rupees on the table of the doctor and said, "We must give you something." "No, no. What are you doing? I did not help you in digging out grain in lentils. The government has allotted me first class residential quarters and pays me a good salary. So what for are you giving me? Take back your money."

Sinath said, "What service shall I render unto you?"

"Yes, if sometime there is some work suited to your tastes, I shall send for you because I consider you my own men, but no money now. Still if you insist on giving something, put it into the charity-box. It will be used for the needy. Those who can, should thus help the poor. The greater and nobler service (slightly smiling) is that you must not break heads again so as to be hospitalised. The beds and medicines for you could have served some other more needy patient."

Both felt ashamed of themselves.

Sinath said, "What you have said is quite right. We shall be careful in future and never forget your sage counsel."

Both left the hospital, healed both physically and mentally. At its gate Sugani Brahmani was sitting with a bundle and a box. As soon as they went out of the gate she accosted them. Both of them looked back but Isar could not recognise her. Sinath, being a little nearer, said, "Are you Sugani Dadi?"

"Yes, I am she."

Sinath looked at her once again with a fixed gaze. Her eyesight was dim, and the eyeballs were pressed within. Her face was pale.

She looked dejected and slightly ill too. He said, "Grandma, you look very much emaciated. You must be on the right side of fifty- six."

"Yes, your honour. Earlier my blood was hot. The climate of the village was salubrious. The food of bread and 'Rabari' was healthy. In Calcutta there was none of those three things".

"Why did you leave Dhanji's service?"

"Where else could I go? I was with Dhanji."

Sinath looked at her and sat beside her. Isar and Sugana proceeded forward. Sinath said, "I fail to understand what you mean."

Breathing deeply she said, "O wise one! Dhanji is not in your village alone. His likes are everywhere in the world. Our country has no dearth of them. Similarly there is not one Sugani but many. It was really Dhanji himself who sent me to Calcutta to serve one of his close relations. As we are, so are they. The Calcuttans surpass others. I laboured for years at Dhanji's and again for years in Calcutta. I had stayed with two rich people."

"Why did you leave Calcutta? What was your salary there?"

"What they gave me should be within your ken."

"He has given me gout and an understanding of their trickery. He has taken the light of my eyes and the water of my hard work. The whole day I cooked food. When I suffered from pain in the legs, he bid me good-bye. The details I will tell you later. My story is long."

"What are your plans for the present?"

"Now I'll accompany you to the village."

"From where have you come now?"

"It's many days since I returned from Calcutta. These days I have been here. I saw my daughter. I came hither when I heard of you. This would save me about five rupees on account of fare. We will be together all along. It will thus be an additional advantage.

"You are ill. You should have better taken treatment here and stayed with your daughter for some days. What is the use of going to the village? No grain will be burnt there in your absence."

"Why shall I suffer taunts from my daughter and son-in-law? If I do not go to the village, I shall be guilty in the eyes of God.I must go, otherwise I would not have left Calcutta."

"Tell me everything frankly."

"That I'll do, but let us move away a little from the footpath. Better ask for the cart."

At some distance the cart was under a thorny tree. Sinath himself drove it. As Sugani could not get up herself, Sinath took her in his arms and put her in the cart. Sinath turned back to stay a while under the shade of the tree.

Isar said, "In less than an hour I shall be back. I have to see my sister whose husband had desired me to meet them at home." Sugana said, "Then why shall I not take some salt, chillies and jaggery to save the trouble of their being pounded at home". Both of them went.

Sugani and Sinath were now sitting in the cart. Sugani took out a card from her box. She said, "I have received it today. Just read it."

"Sinath read," Regards to Sugani Mai from Lakhan Kahar. I am well with your kind blessing. I, too, have given up the job and taken two buffaloes and a cow in Howrah. Hanumania also has gone home to plant vegetables in his two-bigha land which is duly watered. He was sick of his dirty job. Your Seth is at the police station today, since in his godown two stolen bales were seized. Do in the village what I told you. Reply you must. You are like my mother. I can never forget you."

Sugani said, "It was Lakhan who got me released from the jail."

Sinath said, "How did all this happen?"

"Both of them stayed in a small cell situated in the lower part of the closed locality. It was dark since bulbs are not provided for. I got acquainted with them. We thus stayed there for three years. Lakhan used to cleanse utensils at the Seth's house. He did this job at several other places in the ward. He was a straightforward man and in his thirties.

Both of them had fallen ill for about ten days twice or thrice. I used to prepare tea for them at night and did some other chores as was needed, in my spare time. They treated me as their mother. This year when I suffered from gout, the Seth's wife said to me, "It will be good for you to go to your village now. It will be hard for you to continue here."

I said, "Who will give me shelter if I do not return to my village? I shall not force myself upon you and so please pay me my dues."

The Seth looked into the account book and said, "You owe sixty rupees to us but it does not matter. Now that you are taking leave of us, we will also secure a railway ticket for you".

"I was flabbergasted to hear it, for I had hoped to receive some substantial sum."

"I said, 'Please let me know my monthly salary.'

The Seth said, "Rs. 250/- for six years and 300/- for the subsequent six years annually. Food and clothing was free. Twice or thrice we sent you on pilgrimage at our cost."

"I wondered how I was put under such a heavy debt. At a little distance Lakhan heard it all. He came nearer and said, "Cooking for fifteen persons, tea and milk at different times, her being kept busy with cooking work the whole day and all this, O God, for twenty-five rupees! None will do even for a hundred'. The Seth said, 'Do your work without poking your nose in others' affairs!'

"This is my own affair because she is my mother. I cannot tolerate such injustice. I'll call Hanumania and all our ward people will assemble here to see that you do not exploit a poor person'.

The Seth said, 'You take your wages. You were not instrumental in getting her appointed'. 'Then I quit'.

Lakhan said to me, 'You have served them for twelve years and never cleared the accounts. How simple-minded you are!'

I replied, 'Every Year I asked the Seth for accounts but he would tell me not to worry about it and take money as and when needed. I used to send 'every year cloth costing about Rs. 125/- and another Rs. 100/- in cash to my daughter. I never knew what sum exactly I took from him. Some three times or so when I fell ill I had to spend for a little milk and medicines from my own pocket'.

Lakhan said, "Whatever you spent is all right, but what justification is there to fix your monthly salary at this paltry sum?"

Sugani became silent as if she was reclining.

She said again, "I told the Seth that some others work in the ward. Their work is less than mine and yet they are paid sixty rupees per month whereas you seem to favour me by paying twenty- five chips'. The Seth said, 'Talk to Dhanji in this regard. All this was settled with him'. I said, 'I was not sold to you by him. I work under you and you ask me to talk to Dhanji!' The Seth kept mum. Lakhan and his brothers came in the evening. The brother was sharper than Lakhan. He said, "Seth, there must be no bungling in her account. We are many people to plead for her cause. We are not afraid of being imprisoned. In no case we will let you suck her blood." The Seth knew that if he intended mischief, he would get some school-going child of his kidnapped. So he said, "Well, I fix her salary at the rate of forty. I am paying her two thousand rupees and it clinches the matter." But he said, 'This money you are paying as wages. It's no charity', "I told him not to prolong the matter. I was paid Rs. 2000/- but all had sullen faces and there was nothing like good-bye. I spent the night with Lakhan. He asked me about my future plans. On saying that I would go to my daughter he suggested 'No, mother. You once said that in your village there are men and women like you who are exploited. So you go home and not to your daughter. Cook garlic in the preparation of rice and milk boiled together. Take it and see that you are cured of gout. Do not let them exploit women like you. See that they are given full wages. Only on this assurance we will let you go, otherwise stay with us and we will serve you'. He did not let me speak and himself continued, 'Mother, live manfully so long as you have to live. The world will be there even when we are dead and gone'. I assured him that I would act up to his advice."

"Now tell me, Sinath, whether I should accompany you or live under constraint with children in the city. The world and its ways are not of much interest to me now."

Sinath looked at her with transparent eyes. That she had firm faith was clearly visible from her face. He mused, "This poor woman's essence has been squeezed mercilessly. Her small and soft hair on the body must have hundreds of wounds inflicted on them." He said to her, "Grandma, having listened to your tale I quite agree with you. Rest assured that I shall serve you to the best of my capacity."

Sugani said, "So far as food is concerned, I can pat four pots of cow-dung into cakes but I must not be tied to any person whatsoever."

"But grandma, on the one hand, the Seth sent you on pilgrimages and on the other hand charged for your milk and medicines!"

"I know the mystery of pilgrimages. The entire family would visit temples and shrines, and I, left at home, would cook food in the morning and evening and would give tea and milk to the children at different times. In the noon again the tea was boiled for everybody. Wherever we went, I did take bath twice at the wharf. Beyond that I never visited any temple nor kept company with the holy people. My pilgrimage was no more than 'blowing the hearth' Sinath, I do not mind what was given or not given to me. The seminal point is that they are too selfish to mind others' sufferings. Servants, in their eyes, are made of wood. Their business smacks of dirt. Earlier, the Seth's elder brother had been arrested in Viratnagar because of illegal trafficking in clothes."

From a distance Isar and Sugana were seen coming. Sinath said, "you have returned very late. The sun is about to set."

Isar said, "What marriage have we to attend now? My sister prepared a special diet which we thought we would all be eating in the cart and thus the path would be shortened. We will now reach in the night comfortably."

Sinath said, "Come on now. Let the god Ganesha make our journey safe!"

And the cart moved.

14

Soon enough they left the city about one and a half miles behind. As the cart sped forward, all the three passengers felt happy indeed. Sinath said, "How do you like the idea of our going first to Surdas and thence to our homes?"

"This is what I was contemplating."

It was the third day of the first half of 'Fagun'—the sky was clear. Many stars were hanging from there but not one tended to fall. Sinath asked the Dadi to lie down on one side, assuring her that it would be more comfortable than a third class compartment.

"I know the travails of journey. On my back journey from Calcutta in the overcrowded compartment I had all but died. It is the rich who enjoy train journeys. Now I must rest, since I am free from the routine work of cooking."

"In Calcutta there must be some other persons from our side."

"There are many of whom some decorate rich women's palms with myrtle powder while some others do miscellaneous chores. They are like me, cooking food here and there, thus eking out their livelihood. I have seen many men who seldom visit their home."

"Why is it so?"

"They have their farms here but have little love for this soil.They salute the rich in flattering terms. Such spiritless persons are in their constant attendance, sirring them all the time."

"Grandma, such is the world and its ways. Mosquitoes at a window- site are contented only there. Let them be, but you breathe freely in our unpolluted atmosphere." While talking, she started dozing. Sinath said, "Wrap yourself in this light blanket for an hour or so. Let it serve as your bed."

She said that she could not sleep many nights, but now, the moment she lay down she slept.

Sinath mused, "She must not have had such a comfortable sleep any day during her long stay in Calcutta. Such a life-giving breeze never blows in Eden Garden or Victoria. On lawn-grass there are sputum, discharge from noses, husks of groundnuts, coverings of pungent and spicy things, as also waste papers defiled by eating. The worst is the smoke issuing from vehicles like trains and buses. But Dadi luckily was saved from such harrowing experience."

The night was young and below the eastern sky a round bright thing was seen rising. The darkness was gradually disappearing. The night was pleasant and the wind soothing. On the way was a water-hut where they quenched their thirst and stayed for ten minutes. But Dadi did not even open her eyes, as if she was recovering without any medicine.

The laughing sand, huge embankments on four sides, separated sand-dunes, goats, bushes and other trees are all quiet. The camel was moving at an even speed. There was nothing he was not familiar with. It was about 5.30 A.M. The small hours of the morning were somewhat chilly. Sinath noiselessly covered his Dadi's body with his blanket. She slept care-free as though in a trance.

Isar said, "Haven't we reached quite close to our fields? We can see them distinctly from here".

Sinath said, "Why not drop at our fields then?"

"What is there to eat at present?"

"Let us go to the boundary and have a tussle once again."

Isar felt a little embarrassed. He said, "Enough of altercations. The earlier fire is not yet quite extinguished and you want to ignite another one. Let us cultivate the land afresh and have faith in our hard work!"

"God willing, let us also free such people as might be in the grip of evil-minded persons. It shall be a good augury to bring together persons of our likes and temperament to effect the desired progress in our society. Even pigs and dogs fill their bellies but will we, human beings, stop at that? Get down the cart and let us go to our fields after so many months."

Sinath asked Sugana to join them. He took the camel a little farther from the path and tied it to a wild tree. He followed them like a shadow but with a lathi in his hand. Isar became apprehensive. He mused. "How to trust a Jat? I am unarmed and fear that Sinath might kill and throw me into a pit. There cannot be any greater and better time for taking vengeance." His hair stood on end and again he said to himself, "How can Sinath act like a crow? Had he really wanted to kill me, he could have despatched me the very same day. And if I am to be killed like this it is but right, because I sowed the wind and must now reap the whirlwind. He dashed against a cluster and was about to fall when Sinath held him up and said, "What accounts for your absent- mindedness? Why do you stumble like this?"

They soon ascended the embankment and reached exactly the same intended spot.

"Isar, this was the place."

"Yes."

"Then take your dhoti above the ankles and be ready." Isar mused, "There can be no rapport between "Jat and me". He said, "What will you do?"

"We will have a wrestling match."

"At present what wrestling and with whom?"

"Don't fear. We are ourselves. Sugana, give me a *lathi*." Isar was anxious to know what lay in store for him and how fatal it could be. But he spoke not a word. Sinath drew a line and said to Isar, "You come from that side uttering Kabaddi, Kabaddi and I from the other side. Sugana, take the *lathi* to act as referee."

Isar was still more apprehensive. He said, "No, you come first."

It was a bright night and silence reigned everywhere. The stars were, however, in a hurry for respite. In the western sky the moon was sighted coursing fast. There were gusts of cold wind. It seemed that they stopped their movement to see their play.

"So I come. Kabaddi, Kabaddi." The desolate place in the jungle became vocal.

"Thakurji will help. Kabaddi, Kabaddi. Take this, here I hit," but Sinath held his arm against it and said, "Where did you hit? I am living still! Let us move, for the play is over."

Sugana, dumb-like, was watching the whole show. On the other side, the old woman was now awake. She sat silent, like Mother India, as if disappointed because of the rank selfishness of her children and their rash actions. Their race for self- gratification was repulsive.

Sinath said, "Isar, we might have died but did not. We are immortal sons of the soil." Isar even now was not quite at ease, for a black spot was still rankling in him, but soon after it was all washed away in the pure water of the Ganges as it were.

Isar said, "Mistrust breeds suspicion. It's faith and trust that works and stays. The least doubt is hurtful and may prove disastrous any time."

The cart was moving forward. The cloud was pale. The beautiful dawn shall be followed by her father, the sun, who will never be able to overtake her, because the two are destined not to meet, like parallel lines. Even then this is their daily play which the Earth relishes to her heart's content.

The moon became pale in the west. The stars were about to set. Sinath said, "Isar, the rise of one but the other being dull-coloured is extremely pleasant because such is the way of nature. If only the world could follow this pattern. Here, the moment someone rises, the others pull his legs down."

The birds' chirping was sweet to the ears. Houses in the village and trees were gladdening the hearts of both because they were revisiting the surroundings after a lapse of some months. Dadi's joy knew no bounds.

Dhanji was seen washing his hands. Seeing them seated together, he wondered how these contraries could meet. He stood up and said, "Is Sinath here?" Sinath did not respond. The Seth said, "Why do you not speak?"

"Your Honour, the Sinath that you knew is dead. This new Sinath you perhaps do not know. This is why I did not speak."

"What makes you say so?"

"What is the price of a man? In this village and outside, the price cannot be more than Rs. 2,000/- as you know well enough. In the struggle for chairs it might be two lacs. The moment currency notes are offered, there is bound to be a clash. But he who does mean work furtively, is exposed sooner or later."

"I was very much worried and went many times to your house to enquire after your welfare."

"This politics is of a higher order still. Such things happen on a high pedestal of politics. A man in the crowd cannot comprehend it. If you enquired after me, it must be your parental care and affection."

Isar said, "This money grows and blossoms. Let Sinath disagree, but I am obliged to you. But for you I would have been dead. An ungrateful person is a wretch." Sinath said, "He is no enemy of mine. I want him only to smell the earth which is not possible by mere accumulation of wealth."

The cart moved further. The Seth was stupefied. He was uneasy and reflective. He was thinking as to how their separation could be brought about.

The sun's first rays shone forth in the entire village. People started their morning work. Both of them got down the cart and proceeded to their locality. The old woman in the cart was to go home.

There was a small, old but cemented cell. In front there was a rectangular seat. The two were walking very slowly. They heard a sweet sound to the accompaniment of tanpura. Standing outside, they listened to a devotional song in Raga Kanhara.

"Without form, line, quality, means and protection, O Man! where are you wandering? Incomprehensible are you in all ways, hence Surdas sings in praise of God, who is possessed of such attributes."

No sound is heard now as if the chord has been snapped all of a sudden. The Tanpura was placed erect in a corner. Surdas was sitting on a gunny-bag. A half-woven chair was beside him. He took it in his hand. It must be from the school or Panchayat. They moved a little forward. A blind person's hearing power is very keen. Surdas knew that some persons were nearby. He said, "Who are you?"

Both touched his feet, to which he objected.

"We are Isar and Sinath."

"When did you come?"

"Just now and straight here without going home."

"You have done very well. Are you all right?"

"Yes, with your blessing."

"I cannot see your figure and what need is there to see you thus? I am very happy to see you united and speaking with one voice."

He stopped for a minute and then said, "It is your understanding and rapport, certainly not my blessing."

Sinath said, "All these days we could hardly appreciate your nature. You stayed a little aloof. Now I will pay you your dues with interest and something additional too. Even then I shall always remain indebted to you."

"I am blind and dependent. Though I cannot see, I worship God with attributes. I adore neither money nor attributeless God. The man who works hard and honestly, who has renounced his ego and jealousy and who believes in common humanity is my kind. I live to attain what can be best in man. If you realise yourself, there is little need to understand me. I am born with the feeling of unity of mankind. What money do you owe to me?"

Sinath said, "The money that you paid on my behalf."

"When did I give you money? Whatever money I gave was my delight. It was for my satisfaction. Did you ever ask me for money?"

"No, Sir."

"If somebody who does not need money, what shall we say of him? He who thus throws money will not demand it of anybody nor does he really need it."

"It is your greatness, but the money paid by you must be given to you by me."

"Again you do not see the root but are only moving round the leaves of a tree.The altercation was not between two individuals. It might have developed into a class conflict between Jats and Rajputs. There are many to fan the communal fire. Two parties come into conflict in season and out of season. In that flare-up many innocent lives are lost whereas some others revel. The village is thus divided into groups. Some selfish persons sow the seed of discord and shortsighted people fall for it. Such a pernicious seed must be nipped in the bud and replaced by a couple of smiling flowers of reconciliation. If this happens in our society with no rancour, my native delight is multiplied fourfold. I have more than compensation for the money in question."

Surdas became silent for a minute and then continued, "You know that I have no wife or children. If I sleep with money, somebody may be tempted to strangle me. What for do I need money. At the most I may keep a five-rupee note for bus fare, the want of which does not fret me, since God has given me legs to walk with, I spend a few years, say, four, in a village. My attempt is to bring the warring factions closer in order to free them from jealousy, acrimony and to make them breathe freely. Where necessary, I give money provided I have it. I have spent about four years in this village. You two have fulfilled my mission in life. Now I shall shift to some other village, for the entire country is mine. It is both broad and long. I will be comfortable wherever I happen to go. Who will forbid me when I want nothing from anybody?"

Both of them listened to him as though spell-bound and looked at him with a steady gaze. Sinath mused, "What a wonderful man he is! What he decides he does guilelessly. All this is writ large on his face." Sinath, slightly hesitant, said, "You may please have some regard for our sentiments too."

"What else have you to say except paying me money?"

"Nothing much."

"Give by all means but only to the needy and never to a man like me who has no needs. Give when and where you think proper and give more than I can, and according to your means. Gifts, like trade, should multiply. The country has been free for about thirty years. Harijans and Muslims can live only when they align themselves with a particular party, otherwise they are finished because of some lurking fear which they entertain in their minds. They are given concessions with the result that they remain distinctly separated from the common populace. No party is greater than the country. First the good of the country and then of the party."

Isar said, "The situation is bad as it is today."

"When there are different parties, one party may stand to gain, but think whether the country as a whole suffers or not."

Sinath said, "It does suffer."

"If the country breaks, mind it. You have eyes to see. Instil faith in labourers. Rise above party politics as far as you can. Not only you, but mankind as a whole should rise and advance in the right direction."

Sinath said, "We will adopt your ways to the best of our ability, but we would very much like to know a little more about you."

"I am before you. Blind I am. I do not discriminate between caste and colour."

"Were you born blind?"

"I was not blind but have been made blind."

"How is it?"

"Don't ask all this now. It is a long story. I shall relate it to you some other time."

"You must have had some caste?"

"My caste is of a labourer. I work hard everyday for six hours which entitles me to food. Since you too are labourers, we belong to the same caste. Now go. Your parents must be waiting for you with their eyes open."

While leaving, he said again, "Just a minute."

Standing on the threshold he said, "The buffalo is yours; you churn buttermilk and yours is the fodder given to animals. If the walls of opposition and faithlessness are firmly drawn between you, you are bound to be crushed. Cream, ghee etc. are taken away from you. My message is that unity is strength. Now you may go."

They went and Surdas took up the half knitted chair to complete the work. It was about 3.30 P.M. Sinath took some steps back to see Surdas once again! He wanted to ask him how he was blinded.

Sinath went back to see Surdas in the evening. In his eyes Surdas was a speaking book. God makes a blind man see what two-eyed persons cannot. God has bestowed upon him the unfailing inner vision. While walking he looked at the trunk of a Pipal tree. Many boys were playing cards there. Some three of them were playing 'Charbhar', and moving pebbles forward and backward. Many old men at a distance were raising circles of smoke from their hubble-bubble. He found the room of Surdas chained. On opening the gate, he noticed that there was no tanpura, no chair, no gunny-bag. It was deserted like a body bereft of soul. He might have gone to the village but he was told that he had left by the noon bus but nobody was aware of his destination. Sinath felt sorry not to find him but he was all praise for him. He mused, "Blind he was, but he distributed sight; Sudama he was but his hand was always generous in giving, he slept but was awake, and he was melancholy when awake. He was the Kabir, non-possessive and unattached. Selflessly he always helped others and often at his own cost. He would sew the torn, join the broken and teach his craft to others. One day at this very place he had said, "My lover is awake, how can I sleep? ... Awaken the people to see the follies of parochialism."

Lost in thought he passed by a fence when more words from Surdas rang in his ears, "The buffalo is yours; the fodder is yours but not the cream and ghee, even though all work is done by you." He mused, "That Surdas is dead is our misconception for he is present in the consciousness of all villagers. He shall live amidst us all." He joined a group of labourers.

At Dhanji's shop a couple of customers were purchasing a few articles. On the other side were seated Ramdhan and Nathu Godara. They were in colloquy with the Seth. Mrs. Kataria had been there for canvassing. She had just left after lunch. A little while ago, the verandah had been crowded with people. Nathu had said, "Your Honour, It has got to be admitted that Mrs. Kataria is a bold and fearless woman. She is so very dashing that men lag behind. If she wins this time she will renovate the village."

The Seth said, "The trend seems to be favourable. If nothing else, she will certainly feel obliged to us and should be of help in times of need. After all she wields great power."

Ramdhan said, "I learn that Sinath, Padma and Surdas called on her as self-styled leaders, but she did not let them ascend even the staircase. They were dismissed high and dry. Why should she bank on them still?" The Seth was very pleased to hear it and said, "She is too clever for them."

Now comes Suratia with a turban on his head and a bag in his arm. With folded hands he sat on the threshold of the shop in the verandah. He who does not diagnose a patient on just seeing him, is no physician. Even then the Seth said, "How is it that you have come after such a long time?"

"It is because my mother expired day before yesterday. I have to arrange some boiled wheat. You are my parent. As a pigeon rests on a wall, I rely exclusively on you."

"Now many people of the settlement are wide awake. Why not seek help from them?"

"Let them be. They will care for themselves and their ilk. I have always been under your protection which should continue unabated."

Nathu said, "Those you are talking of are no strangers to me. One is Sinath. The two brothers have two grown-up daughters. He will accomplish a miracle if they are married off. The other is the wiseacre Surdas who is reported to have left bag and baggage today."

The Seth commented, "It's a good riddance. He was a mischief- monger. His mode of speech was as bitter as a swallow wort."

Ramdhan said, "There may be one or two more like him, but they are fickle clouds. Those who, in expectation of rain, put their jars upside down are fools indeed."

Dhanji said, "You have grain enough for two months but the rainy season is still far off. When called, you shake your hand as if you were the Prime Minister's son. Till yesterday I nurtured you with buttermilk and 'rabari' as my own children, and today you have the cheek to say all this."

"Will the Seth chop off my tail. For food I am subservient to none."

"But when God has given you no tail, what is there to be chopped off?"

Ramdhan said, "Chaudhari, you have yet to repay the loan given against your harvest."

Nathu said, "Your grace, you have said that the rainy season is far off, but even otherwise in the life of a householder there is no end to botherations like marriages of sons and daughters, parents' approaching death, condiments, special provision for water after the birth of a child, fever, and not infrequent beatings. You are sons of the goddess of wealth. Can we ever hope to live without your active support?"

Suratia was so wounded in spirit that nothing worse could possibly happen to him. With folded hands he said, "Respected parents, I only prattle and know not how to talk. But what I say is the voice of my conscience. I am the same old Suratia and who else but you will help me in my dire need?"

"Tell me what you want."

He opened his bag and said, "Here are silver ornaments and about three sacks of grain in lentils."

"How many rupees do you need?"

"A thousand will be barely sufficient."

"Then it is difficult to see you through. What about your grass and fodder?"

"I have about six cart-loads of them."

"You should dispose it of, since you have no cows."

"It will be sent here for being cut."

Ramdhan said, "Purakha was just here. Day after tomorrow his son's marriage party is to proceed and he himself has arrived so late for it. He who stays at the village must worship at the shrine."

Nathu said, "Sir, be kind to this boy. I assure you that he is in no way inferior to others."

The Seth put the ornaments inside when Kesaro Kotwal came and said, "Here are two trucks of bush leaves."

Nathu said, "You are lucky indeed. Its price has gone up. In the city the rate varies from Rs. 20 to 22. Hazarimal has this year earned a lot."

"My income this time is just sufficient. The future is hidden from us. Suratia, let us strike this bargain that has come our way. It might be profitable." They all went together.

The Seth said to himself, "A few whimsical persons of the village are arranging basins high up not knowing that even if a single basin lying below is displaced, the whole superstructure shall crumble. The fox is gifted with a thousand tricks which is difficult for them to comprehend."

The sun has set. Suratia's four-pronged wooden implement sorted out a full truck-load leaves so as to make full use of the truck. His head and face were smeared with sand that he could hardly be recognised. His hands and feet were parched with thorns. After the truck was loaded, he gently sought permission from the Seth to go.

"Yes, now you may go but bring tomorrow three sacks of grain in lentils. For grass I'll send carts."

"Yes, Sir."

"Then go."

And the Seth started counting the currency notes in the light of the bulb.